The Goodbye Season

The Goodbye Season

MARIAN HALE

SQUARE
FISH

HENRY HOLT AND COMPANY
NEW YORK

SQUARE
FISH

An Imprint of Macmillan
175 Fifth Avenue
New York, NY 10010
macteenbooks.com

Our books may be purchased in bulk for promotional, educational, or business use.
Please contact your local bookseller or the Macmillan Corporate and
Premium Sales Department at (800) 221-7945 ext. 5442 or by
e-mail at MacmillanSpecialMarkets@macmillan.com.

Library of Congress Cataloging-in-Publication Data
Hale, Marian.
The goodbye season / Marian Hale.
    p.   cm.
Summary: In Canton, Texas, seventeen-year-old Mercy's dreams of a different life than
her mother's are postponed by harsh circumstances, including the influenza epidemic of
1918–19, which forces her into doing domestic work for a loving, if troubled, family.
    ISBN 978-1-250-06285-7 (paperback)   ISBN 978-1-42998-217-7 (ebook)
[1. Coming of age—Fiction.   2. Family life—Texas—Fiction.   3. Household
employees—Fiction.   4. Mothers and daughters—Fiction.   5. Grief—Fiction.
    6. Texas—History—1846–1950—Fiction.]   I. Title.
    PZ7.H1373Goo 2009   [Fic]—dc22   2008050275

Originally published in the United States by Henry Holt and Company, LLC
First Square Fish Edition: 2015
Square Fish logo designed by Filomena Tuosto

1   3   5   7   9   10   8   6   4   2

AR: 5.3 / LEXILE: 850L

For my children,
ALIISA, MICAH, *and* ALLISON.
My sweetest calling, my greatest pride.

The Goodbye Season

"The greater part of our happiness or misery depends on our dispositions and not our circumstances."

MARTHA WASHINGTON

chapter
I

I'M A FIRSTBORN, like my mama and my gramma before me.

"Whether you like it or not, Mercy Kaplan," Mama is always telling me, "the eldest gets called on to do things that don't seem fair."

I cleaned grits from baby Honor's chubby face, then dropped to my knees to mop up the rest of her breakfast. Four-year-old Justice giggled, seeing me scoot around the floor like a hound hunting for scraps, and when I looked up, I saw him wipe his mouth on his sleeve. I grimaced. Another shirt to wash. And for a kid who'll probably never use a scrub board a day in his life.

Mama was right about the curse of being the eldest, and right about another thing, too. None of it was fair.

Charity sat next to Justice at the table, picking over a mound of pinto beans, her grits-smeared bowl pushed back, left for me to clear away. At fourteen, she was only two years younger than me, old enough by far to carry her fair share of chores, but Mama didn't seem to notice.

I gave Justice's sleeve a quick swipe with my rag and snatched Charity's bowl from the table. She shot me a surprised look, full of hurt, then ducked her head and went back to her beans.

I didn't mean to hurt her feelings, but I was tired of picking up after everyone. Getting beans ready for the pot seemed to be the only thing she did well enough to satisfy Mama, a fact that appeared to escape everyone but me. If I hadn't always tried to please, maybe I would've had less work, too.

I felt Mama's eyes on me and tossed her a quick glance. I guess my irritation had shown all over me, because she rested her mending in her lap and gave me a long look. I braced myself for some stinging words, but she didn't say a thing till I'd finished my chores and sat Honor on the floor to play. Then I heard her sigh.

"Remember, Mercy," she said, her words as threadbare as the overalls she was mending. "Each burden comes with its own blessing."

She picked up her needle, leaving me to ponder what that blessing might be and whether I'd be lucky enough to get it in this life or have to wait till the next. There sure hadn't been any reward for all the cleaning, laundry, and tending kids she expected me to do. In fact, I'd come to believe this was all I'd ever get out of life.

Lately, I'd been mulling over the prospect of leaving home. I was old enough, almost seventeen, but hard as I tried, I couldn't see how a girl could break free and make a life for herself without marrying some fool boy. Even if I did manage to find a decent boy my age to marry, how would I keep from ending up like Mama, saddled with four kids, all of us named after virtues, like prayers to God, instead of for grammas and grampas, like everyone else in the world?

Uh-uh. That was *not* going to happen to me. I was not going to be like Mama.

Something waited for me; I could feel it, especially at night, when everyone was asleep. The promise sat on my chest like a big tabby cat, warm and velvety, purring about the happy future that might be mine if I could just figure out how to get there from here. Only how was a Texas sharecropper's daughter supposed to set her sights on something better if she didn't even know what was out there in the world? At least one thing was clear. My life would never be different from Mama's if I married.

When I thought back, it seemed to me there'd always been something standing in the way of better times. Like the war with Germany. "A war to end all wars," everyone said. Papa shipped off to fight the Kaiser like everyone else, and Mama had to work every day, taking in laundry and ironing, to keep enough food on the table. When he was wounded and sent home, we all looked on it like a miracle straight from heaven. Papa was alive, and he was home safe. The last two fingers on his right hand were missing, but he was whole in every other way, and life could be better at last. And for a while, it was.

Early this past spring, we celebrated the chance to share-crop Mr. Gurtry's rich land just outside of Canton. When the rains came and Papa's cotton bushed out green and beautiful, I thought we'd finally reap that blessing Mama was so fond of talking about, but I should've known better. The boll weevils found us, and though we all worked hard to save the crop, in the end there was nothing to do but give up.

By September, Papa had returned Mr. Gurtry's team of mules, and this morning he rode our old Tucker into Canton to look for work. When he finally came home at dusk, something about him had changed. Everything out of his mouth sounded strained and far away, like he'd buried his words so deep he could hardly summon them up anymore. Seeing his cotton crop fail day by day had worried deep shadows around his eyes, and tonight they seemed even darker. The kids swarmed around his knees, trying to cheer him up, but nothing helped for long, not even Honor's crooked grins. Papa's brow soon furrowed again, and the shadows deepened.

Papa ate his beans slow, his arms resting around his bowl after each bite. When we were done, I cleaned up the supper dishes, hoping he'd read to us awhile, make everything feel right again, but it was clear he had too much on his mind. I couldn't help wondering how things went in town, but I knew he'd speak of it only to Mama.

I pulled Honor's nightgown over her head and handed her to Mama. I guess she'd spoiled us all, one by one, singing us to sleep. Even now, as old as I was, her songs could comfort me like nothing else. I pushed Justice up the loft ladder and heard her voice, whisper-soft, behind me.

"Hush, little baby, don't say a word."

The slow *creak-creak* of the rocker kept time with her words.

"Mama's gonna buy you a mockingbird."

In the loft, a gusty wind whistled through cracks in the siding, weaving itself like a ghost through Mama's lullaby, but it did little to lessen the late-summer heat. We changed into our nightclothes, rolled out our pallets, and lay down, already sticky with sweat.

Before long I heard Justice's and Charity's deep breathing behind me. While listening to the rhythmic creak of Mama's rocker, I felt myself drifting away, too. But Papa's voice reached right through the dozy comfort I'd found, and, like a big hand, it snatched me back.

I eased up and glanced behind me, wondering if the kids had roused, too. Hot as it was, Justice had worked his way off his pallet and spooned against Charity's back, tight as a tick on a hound, but they were both still asleep. I lay back down, staring at the way light flickered like fairy wings across the rafters, and soon Papa's words drifted up to me, tangled in the wispy smoke from the kerosene lamp and the blustery heat of a dying summer.

"There's no work for me in town, Lydie," he said.

His words sounded chafed and raw, pulled from some sore place only Papa knew.

"I've gotta leave. There won't be enough food to get us through the winter if I don't."

I heard a muffled sound and knew Mama was trying not to cry.

"Mr. Gurtry said you and the children were welcome to glean his fields. The sweet potatoes and rabbit traps should see you through till I find work and can send money home. If it gets too bad, you can sell old Tucker."

I swallowed hard. We'd eaten a lot of sweet potatoes lately. I wasn't sure I could stomach them morning, noon, and night, but even that wouldn't be as bad as being without Papa.

In a voice so soft I almost missed the words, Mama said, "Don't worry, Jess. We'll be all right."

Papa didn't answer. His silence, thick and heavy, pulled me closer to the rail. I heard him draw a ragged breath and waited for more.

"Lydie," he said, "Mr. Gurtry told me that Beulah Bonner could use someone to help around their place. She said she'd take our Mercy for a while if it would help out."

Papa had spoken the words with such tenderness it took a moment for the meaning to soak in. When it hit me, I sucked in a breath, then covered my mouth, afraid he'd heard. But he hadn't. He went right on talking about the Bonners while every foolish fancy I'd ever had about leaving flew plumb out of my head.

"She can't pay wages, but she said Mercy could work for her keep till I get back for spring planting."

"But, Jess," Mama said, "the Bonner place is twelve miles away, and there'll be only Miz Beulah to watch out for her. A sixteen-year-old girl needs her mother."

"There'll be one less to feed, Lydie. Besides, she'll be seventeen next month, and she's a good girl. She can do this."

The thought of living with strangers squirmed sick inside me. This wasn't the way I'd pictured things at all. I'd always thought that leaving would be *my* doing, not Mama's or Papa's.

I rolled over and peered down at them from the edge of the loft. Papa sat at the table, his face pale as winter butter. Mama, clutching a sleeping Honor, rose from her rocker. "She'll *not* leave," she said.

Papa leaned in to the table and covered his face with his hands. Mama watched, her lips drawn thin and tight, and for a moment, I felt safe. But, like a slender birch in an icy wind, Mama shuddered. She fell back onto her rocker and buried her tears in Honor's nightgown.

I shrank from the edge of the loft and lay back down beside Charity. Mama's sobs had left me numb, inside and out, and empty as Papa's pockets.

chapter
2

I'D NEVER SPENT a night away from home. Not one. That much about my life had always been predictable, and by day's end, no matter where we lived, Charity slept right beside me. I could always count on Mama to use the same wooden mixing bowl and black pot. Her crocheted pineapple tablecloth covered every table we'd ever had, and her four china teacups always sat on a shelf or a mantel alongside Papa's harmonica. I never realized what a good thing all that was till now.

Before daylight, the warm breeze died, and the cabin grew close and quiet. I lay there listening to myself breathe, and when I couldn't stand the sound another minute, I pulled off my nightgown, dressed, and headed for the loft ladder.

Guided by stars and the outline of trees against a sleeping sky, I made my way to the creek and eased myself onto the rocks I'd nestled together when we'd first arrived. The stony seat was cool and hard. It would be here long after I was gone, long after we were all gone. The creek bubbled its agreement and churned through the woods.

I felt foolish. All this time I thought leaving was what I'd wanted, but being without Mama and Papa, missing out on

Honor's giggles and Justice's shines, wasn't what I wanted at all. And what about Charity, with her long chestnut braids and big doe eyes? I remembered the hurt look she gave me when I snatched her bowl from the table, and guilt skittered through me, full of sharp edges.

Why did I do things like that? I didn't resent her nearly as much as I let on. She was my sister, my best and only friend. We told each other things we'd never breathe to another soul.

Unlike me, Charity had known all along what she wanted to do when she grew up. She wanted to write books. She'd filled every sheet of paper in the house with her stories, and I was the only one she'd shown them to. For my sixteenth birthday, she'd spent weeks embroidering a bookmark for me, sneaking off to the barn to work so she wouldn't spoil the surprise. And just days ago, she'd spoken up for me, sharing the blame when Mama fussed about letting the water barrel get too low.

I picked up a smooth, round pebble and rolled it in the palm of my hand. I should've been a better sister to her.

Charity was the only one who knew how badly I wanted my life to be different from Mama's. We'd talked way into the night many times, whispering about the girls we'd known who had let themselves get swept away by handsome, sweet-talking boys promising the moon. It seemed to me that Mama hadn't been much different. I knew she loved Papa, but I often wondered if she'd ever regretted her decision to marry. After all, she had a fine education. She could've done anything she wanted. Why would she let herself get buried under endless piles of diapers, dishes, and laundry? True, she was quick to put on a smiling face most days, but I figured she had to know we'd never have more than we had right now, and that scared me. So far, my life had been as empty as Mama's, barren as Papa's cotton fields, and I wasn't at all sure I could change it. The only thing I knew was that I *had* to be smarter than Mama or I'd end up just like her, and then I'd never know what might've been.

I tossed the smooth stone toward the creek just to hear it plop, but it missed and hit the pebbled bank. It was too dark to see it tumble down, but I felt it rattling against the growing emptiness inside me.

"Life's always gonna bring change, Mercy," Mama told me long ago. "It's up to each of us to get shed of old regrets and watch for the good coming."

The trifling bit of good I'd seen lately could hardly be measured, but as much as I wanted to blame someone, I really couldn't point a finger at Mama or Papa. No one had worked harder than they had.

I closed my eyes, already knowing what to watch for. I saw the creek grow full from soft spring rains, and sunshine sparkle across the rushing water like rhinestones I'd seen in a store window once. The air, full of honeybees and shimmering dragonflies, smelled sweet with the new green of a plentiful crop. I breathed in the picture and felt it loosen the knot inside me. Papa's spring planting wasn't so far away. I'd be back home in time to help him sow the seeds, and then maybe I could figure out what the world had waiting for me.

When I finally opened my eyes, morning had crept across the land in feathery, russet golds. I needed to get back home. Mama would be worried.

I hurried to the cabin and heard a distant *whack* split the early quiet. Others followed, echoing across the fields. I knew the bin at the back of the cabin was already full, but Papa was out there somewhere, cutting more wood.

Mama stood at the table when I came in, pouring the last of our flour into her wooden mixing bowl. I wondered if she would tell me what she'd learned last night, but she just nodded toward the black kettle on the stove.

"Hurry and eat, now. I need you to take Charity and Justice up to Mr. Gurtry's fields, see if you can dig up enough potatoes to last us awhile."

"Yes, ma'am." I pulled a still-warm potato out of the pot and swallowed hard. I was sick of boiled sweet potatoes, but I was hungry. I bit into the sticky orange flesh and watched Mama add salt and water to her flour. I figured she must be making hardtack for Papa's journey. I waited, thinking she'd say something about his leaving, about my working for the Bonners, but she just kept on mixing, never once looking up from her bowl.

Charity returned with two buckets of fresh water, and while she fetched tow sacks from the barn, I rolled up three of the six remaining sweet potatoes in a cup towel. I grabbed a ladle for dipping from the creek, poked the handle through the knotted cloth, and swung the bundle across my shoulder.

Justice wrapped his short arms around Mama's skirt and peered up at her through ginger-brown locks. "Mercy says we're gonna see who can find the most taters today, and I think it's gonna be me."

Mama smiled, wiped her hands on her apron, and pushed the ringlets from his forehead. "I wouldn't be at all surprised." She leaned close to his ear. "You're bound to win," she whispered. "You're a lot closer to the ground than she is."

He beamed a triumphant smile at me.

When Charity showed up, we herded Justice out of the house and up the long footpath to the road. Before we reached the bend in the trail, I glanced back and saw Mama still standing in the doorway, watching. I couldn't help but wonder why she hadn't said anything about my leaving, but I was glad of it. Her silence had kindled a spark of hope in me. Maybe something had changed. Maybe I wouldn't have to go after all.

The sun crept above the tree line, taking the dew with it, and our bare feet kicked up dust that drifted in the still morning like fog. Justice talked about trapping rabbits, while Charity rattled on and on about *Jane Eyre* by Charlotte Brontë, her latest favorite book.

"Wouldn't it be wonderful if one of us actually found a job as governess for a man like Mr. Rochester?" she asked.

I tossed her a cynical look. " 'Governess' is just a fancy word for taking care of someone else's kids, teaching them their lessons and cleaning up after them. Heaven knows we get enough of that already, Charity. Besides, I thought you wanted to write books."

"Well, I do, but who wouldn't want to marry someone as romantic as Mr. Rochester and live in a mansion like Thornfield Hall? You know, Mercy, with Mama's schooling, she could've done exactly what Jane Eyre did."

I gave her a scornful huff. "I guess Mama had other ideas about what she wanted."

Though I didn't let on, I did agree with Charity. Surely Mama could've chosen from a dozen other possibilities. Instead, she'd picked this one. For the life of me I couldn't understand why. But thanks to her merciless home schooling and Papa's penchant for making books as worthy of his hard-earned money as seed, they'd managed to see that Charity and I had gotten a proper education, despite our never setting foot in a schoolhouse. It was a gift. One I sure wouldn't waste like Mama did.

Charity had been reading since she was barely five—and no wonder, with that stubborn streak of hers. Back then, she couldn't stand that I got to take turns reading stories with Mama and Papa and she didn't. She wanted a turn, too, and wouldn't let up till she could read well enough to get one. Justice had proven to be a lot like her. He badgered us this summer till we taught him how to recognize his letters by sight. It wouldn't be long now before he was reading, too.

I glanced across the fallow land around me, thinking about our first day here. "See that," Papa had said, pointing to a line of trees that meandered as far as the eye could see. "Good soil—all of it—hugged up against the creek like that."

He pulled Mama from the wagon that day and waltzed her right out into the fields, singing in that deep voice of his, swirling Mama's skirt over the rich earth. Then he threw back his head and laughed. I can hear it still, that booming laugh, echoing across the land, putting toothy grins on all our faces. I can feel the way it swelled inside me, too, full of promise. Funny how some things stick in a person's head clear as day.

The Gurtry fields lay over the far ridge, not even an hour's walk away. Though Mr. Gurtry owned several sections of the valley, age had sucked away his strength. At least, that's what I thought till I heard that his wife had died a few years back.

Mama said that sometimes losing a wife of forty years can wear a man's will too thin for him to go on, and I guess it was so. Mr. Gurtry soon decided he couldn't keep farming so many acres. He let all his help go, took in families like ours to share-crop, and, this past spring, planted only a small section of his land in sweet potatoes. Papa planted cotton.

Late rains had packed Mr. Gurtry's fields, but a few dry, sunny days had left a hard crust over the still-damp soil. We broke through to the wet, sandy earth beneath, but it clung to the potatoes and was downright stubborn about giving up what was left of the harvest.

After we had searched through the rain-melted rows for a few hours, an ache took root in my back like a wild briar and spread upward to my neck and shoulders. I knew Charity must be feeling it, too. Poor little Justice had already tuckered out and fallen asleep in a small patch of weeds. I stretched, pulled my sweat-sticky dress from my legs, and heard Charity groan.

"Can't we stop awhile, Mercy? I'm hungry."

Justice raised his head and rubbed his eyes. "Me, too."

"You're always hungry," I told him, but I nodded anyway and told Charity to take him down to the creek. I picked up the bundle I'd carried from home and trudged after them so we could eat our midday meal in the shade.

By late afternoon, we'd gathered a full sack of sweet potatoes, and I sat under a big red oak to sort out the most damaged ones. These would need to be eaten first. We washed the mud-caked potatoes in the creek, filled the bags according to what each of us could carry, and started back.

The road always seemed to stretch twice as long on the way home. While my feet beat a rhythm against the hard-packed dirt, I thought about last night, hoping that Mama would be smiling when I got home, that I wouldn't have to hear what I'd been dreading.

When we finally rounded the bend and the cabin came in sight, a sinking feeling hit me. I saw Mama gathering in clean clothes from the line—Papa's pants, his two good work-shirts, and my two dresses. I glanced toward the back of the house. The contents of the woodbin had more than doubled in size.

Papa sat on the front steps, looking tired and sore, working on a rabbit trap.

Justice ran the last few yards and tumbled into his arms. "We found lots of taters, Papa. Big ones."

Papa hugged him close. "You did a good job." His eyes closed for a long moment before he finally released Justice and moved to the middle of the step. Patting the weathered board on either side of him, he said, "Come sit by me, all of you. There's something I need to tell you."

I sat on Papa's left, but I couldn't bring myself to look at him. I turned my eyes toward the horizon instead, where a flock of geese painted a winged angle across the evening sky, and for a moment, I wished I was up there with them. I waited, watching the birds' soundless flight, too high for their calls to carry, too high for them to hear Papa's words.

He spoke to Justice first, and his voice wavered, soft with promise but full of the shadow of his leaving. When he finished telling Charity how important it would be to help take care of old Tucker, Papa lifted his head and turned pain-glazed eyes in my direction. I felt my hand disappear in his warm grasp and watched his lips move in soundless explanation. I didn't want to hear, but before long, his words wormed their way through my head, and emptiness settled inside me.

There was too little food.

I would have to go. Like Papa. Tomorrow.

Where's the firstborn blessing now, Mama? I wanted to shout at her. But one look at the misery in her eyes and I knew I could never hurt her with such selfish words.

She touched my shoulder, and I felt her hand tremble.

chapter
3

THE NIGHT SEEMED ENDLESS, full of stifling heat and fitful sleep. Justice whimpered, and Charity kicked till her pallet lay twisted around her legs. I straightened it and waited.

Morning finally gilded the washboard-size window in the loft. The kids scrambled down to breakfast, but I took my time dressing and braiding my hair. Mama's long-ago words whispered to me while I packed my belongings in a rose-print flour sack. "Look for the good," she'd said, and I wanted to. But it was hard.

While Papa said his goodbyes to Mama and the kids, I checked the loft again, knowing full well that I hadn't forgotten anything, but feeling drawn to its warmth, like the birds I'd seen winging south. Pallets were rolled up on the floor, bundled like wheat, and Justice's and Charity's few belongings sat on shelves above pegs that held their clothes. A notebook diary and a stack of old school tablets sat on Charity's shelf. She'd carefully erased the homework from all the pages and filled them again with her stories. Justice's shelf held an old arrowhead and a tin soldier dressed in red. Mine was empty. I stared at the space where my books, comb, and blue ribbon had been, then turned and climbed down the ladder.

Everyone had finished their goodbyes and gone outside to wait for me. From the doorway, I saw Papa standing in the yard, his pack and bedroll strapped to his back. He had far to go, with no assurance of work ahead. I wished we could walk together, at least part of the way, but the Bonners' farm lay in the opposite direction from the one he'd be traveling.

Mama, her eyes red but dry, held Honor on her hip, and when she kissed me on the cheek, I felt her lips quiver. Justice clung to her, half hidden behind the folds of her skirt. I nuzzled Honor's neck, breathing in the baby-soft sweetness of her, and roughed up Justice's hair just to see him grin. Then I turned to Charity. Her face bore a wretchedness only a sister would understand, and I figured I'd carry that picture of her till the day I came home again. She hugged me a bit too tight, making my eyes sting with tears, then stepped back.

Papa had waited, watching. When I finished my goodbyes, he held out his arms, and I rushed to him.

He was warm and smelled of Mama's soap. I leaned my head against his chest, listening to the soft sounds of his breathing, and felt his arms tighten.

"Don't be worrying over me, Papa," I whispered. "Spring's not so far away."

chapter
4

HOW IS IT that a body can feel so alone, so dead inside, and yet birds still chirp, locusts keep singing, and the sun just goes on shining like nothing in the world has changed?

I stopped in the middle of the road and looked back the way I'd come. Papa was most likely well on his way. If I turned around now, another half-hour's walk would take me right home again.

I wondered what Mama would say if I showed up at the door. There was a good chance she might not be mad at all. She hadn't wanted me to leave anyway.

I sat down at the edge of the road, pondering the idea, while I watched ants scurrying over a dead grasshopper, dismantling him, carrying him off piece by piece, storing him away for the winter. Unlike ants, we didn't have much of anything stored up for harsher times. If I turned around now and went back home, how could I be sure there would be enough food for us all?

I pictured Honor crying because her bowl was empty, and shut my eyes tight, trying to squeeze the awful image out of my head.

Papa was right. I had to go.

I stood up and brushed off the dust. My foolish hope had left me empty all over again, and there was nothing I could do about it but head on down the road, away from home, away from Mama and the kids.

The walk to the Bonners' farm would take most all day, which gave me plenty of time to think about what was ahead. It was hard to imagine what my life would be like, but I did remember seeing Miz Beulah and her husband that first day we stopped to ask directions to Mr. Gurtry's farm. She'd given us a big grin, and I smiled right there on the road at the recollection of it. But Mr. Bonner had just stood there, shoulders stooped, a hard glare in his eyes, while he stared at all us kids and our loaded wagon.

I slowed my steps, remembering how the old man's frown had shivered through me. It was easy to see he didn't care too much for sharecroppers, and I told Mama so.

"You can't always tell a body's inner spirit by just looking," Mama whispered back. "Sometimes you have to wait for a heart sign before you can tell what's inside."

I asked her what that would be, and she said, "It's different each time, but you're a smart girl. You'll know when it happens, and you'll know when it happens to you, too."

"To me?"

"Everyone's got to know their own heart, Mercy. Just watch for the signs, and they'll show you what's right and good."

I stared at her, wondering how that could be. I sure hadn't

seen any signs in myself, but I thought I might've felt something with Miz Beulah that long-ago morning. Maybe that's what heart signs were. She'd hobbled across the porch to greet us, her soft bulk bouncing with each step, her wrinkles pushed back by a big smile. She flapped her apron at a red hound she called Banks and shooed him from the steps. I'd seen something in her eyes that day that I'd liked right off—something safe—and before long, I decided it might be good to hang on to that part of the memory and just hope for the best.

When the sun sat high in the sky and sweat had beaded up all over me, I stopped to cool off and eat my dinner under a big shade tree. While I unwrapped my sweet potato, a shiny black Model T came speeding down the road. It held the first people I'd seen all day. I stood up to watch, but it quickly disappeared in a cloud of dust. I went back to my meal, wondering if I'd ever get to ride in an automobile like that. I suspected it might scare me a bit, going that fast, but there was no doubt it would be exciting.

I finished off my sweet potato, went back to the road, and picked up my pace some, figuring that every step I took would only shorten the distance between now and spring.

Shadows lengthened, and by late evening, I topped a small ridge and saw the Bonner farm. It looked much the way it did that first day. Their fields started at the base of the slope and stretched all around the homestead and beyond, almost as far as I could see. To the right of the house stood two ramshackle cabins—for hired help, I reckoned.

Though badly in need of paint, the main house still looked to be a fine place. I squinted against the evening sun, my gaze wandering across the big front porch to the pecan trees, then up to the chimney, where jackdaws sat around the brick edges like black clothespins. My stomach clenched and pitched at what was coming, but there was no help for it except to get this first meeting over and done with.

I started down the rise and saw Banks, the red hound, raise his head in my direction. As I neared, he loped down the porch steps and stood waiting under a leafy fig tree. I watched for a tail wag and was soon rewarded. At least the dog liked me. He let out a halfhearted bark and looked toward the screen door.

Miz Beulah stepped onto the porch and shaded her eyes with her hand. "That you, Mercy Kaplan?"

"Yes, ma'am." I opened the weathered gate and walked up to the porch.

"I wondered if you'd come." The woman eyed me closely. "Well, aren't you a tall one?" She raised a finger and pointed at me. "But that ain't a bad thing. I always wisht I was tall. Sure woulda come in handy all these years."

I wiped my feet, stepped onto a worn plank floor, and followed her past the parlor, straight through to the back of the house. Miz Beulah pointed to a chair, and I sat down at a honey-colored pine table covered with white linen. Embroidered redbirds hopped around the crocheted edge.

She pumped water at the sink and set two glasses on the

table. "You must be tired after that long walk," she said. "Are you hungry?"

I glanced at the icebox sitting in the corner, at the hand pump hanging over the nice white sink, at the worktable with its big tins of flour and sugar and coffee pushed back against the wall. "No, thank you, Miz Beulah. I'm fine for now."

She nodded, eased herself into a chair, and looked right into my eyes. "You ever been away from home before?"

The question surprised me. I hadn't once counted on anyone here being bothered with the feelings of a sixteen-year-old girl. I shook my head. "No, ma'am. Not ever."

She nodded, thoughtful like. "I was younger than you the first time I got farmed out—scared, too, that I might not ever see my mama again."

I flinched, hearing my own fears hanging over the table like that. "Did you?" I asked. "See your mama again, I mean?"

Miz Beulah looked at me, but she didn't answer my question. "You'll do fine, Mercy Kaplan, and it's a fact that we all get to see our mamas again someday."

I sipped the cool water, then emptied the glass. If she'd meant to reassure me, I'd found no comfort in her words.

"I'm afraid you're steppin' into a lot of hard work here," she said, "though I 'spect you're up to it, bein' the oldest and all."

"Yes, ma'am. I can do most anything except make bread as good as my mama's." I gave her an uneasy glance. "But with a little more practice, I'm sure I could do that, too."

She nodded. "That's good, 'cause we're gettin' to be a

pitiful pair, the mister and me." She took a long drink from her glass. "My old knees ain't what they used to be, and Mr. Bonner ain't been hisself, neither. I'm real sorry for your family's misfortune, Mercy, but I'm mighty glad to have a little help."

"Is there something I should be doing now, Miz Beulah?"

"Heavens, no." She leaned on the table and pushed herself up. "You ain't even put your clothes away yet." She grabbed the glass and gave the cloth a swipe with her hand. "Here, put this in the sink for me, and I'll show you where you'll be sleeping."

I did as I was told, then followed Miz Beulah's slow climb to the attic.

"It ain't much," she said, "but the cot and bedding's clean. I took over the spare room downstairs, what with Mr. Bonner's snoring and all, or I woulda put you there." She laughed. "Come to think of it, the attic might be the quietest place in the house."

I stepped into a cramped space that smelled of dust and too many years and looked around me. A small round window had been pushed open in the south gable, letting in a warm breeze. The evening sun streamed in, too, splashing a bright angled light against the rafters. Crates and trunks, picture frames and odd bits of furniture had been pushed back, stacked against the walls, and in the cleared space under the window, I saw the cot Miz Beulah had mentioned, with clean bedding folded at the foot. Leaning next to it was a squatty chest, and on its cracked and peeling surface sat a washbowl and pitcher of water, kerosene lamp and matches, all fighting for their bit of space.

"It's very nice, Miz Beulah. Thank you."

She gave me a pleased smile. "Now, you get settled, and when you come down, we'll work on supper and get to know each other."

"Yes, ma'am," I said, smiling back at her.

"Mr. Bonner is sure gonna be surprised." She chuckled softly to herself. "He didn't think you'd come."

Miz Beulah hobbled out of the room, and when she closed the door behind her, I just stood there, feeling like a thistle seed plucked up in a big wind and blown off to a faraway land. I couldn't imagine lying alone on a cot every night, staring up at that circle of sky, waiting for sleep to come. There'd be no Justice to push up the loft ladder, no Charity chattering beside me in the dark, no lullabies from Mama to soothe away the fears and grumbles of the day.

Standing on my toes, I peered out the round window and glimpsed the long road winding back to Mama and the kids. A yearning for home welled up in my throat so thick and fearsome I wished I'd just choke on it and get all this torment done with. But I didn't, of course. I finally had to turn my back on the promise of home and unpack.

It didn't take long to empty my clothes into a drawer and make up my bed. When I was through, I went downstairs to find Miz Beulah already browning salt pork in a black pot. On the enamel worktable, she'd laid out onions and potatoes. Anxious to please, I picked up the knife she'd set nearby and went to work peeling and chopping.

She looked up at me and smiled. "I can see we're gonna get along just fine."

I smiled back. I wasn't worried about Miz Beulah anymore: I was pretty sure I could keep her happy. But Mr. Bonner was another matter. I glanced out the window, remembering the look he'd given us that first day here, wondering what he'd think when he saw a sharecropper's daughter sitting at his supper table.

chapter
5

AROUND SUNDOWN, I saw Mr. Bonner through the kitchen window. He was making his way in from the fields, and Banks trotted close beside him, his pink tongue dangling from the side of his mouth. Miz Beulah said the men had been working on their fall crop of beets and cabbages. I watched Mr. Bonner give a tired wave to the two young men behind him leading mules. One stopped at the barn to bed down the animals, and the other headed off to one of the shacks sitting not far from the house.

"That's Owen and Garrett Denton," Miz Beulah said when I asked about them. "Brothers. The oldest of nine children, and as good as any mama or papa could wish for. Ever' month they send most all their pay back home to help out."

As soon as Miz Beulah caught sight of her husband washing up outside, she scooped up three bowls and ladled them full of potato soup.

"Set that skillet of cornbread on the table, will you, Mercy? And pour a cup of coffee for Mr. Bonner." She brought the steaming bowls to the table. "He always likes coffee with his supper."

I did as I was told, then hung back by the worktable while he shuffled inside the kitchen door. He slapped his sweat-stained hat on a hook by the screen, sat down at the table, and stared at the third bowl. I watched him stiffen, and a sick wave hit my stomach. He slowly raised his head and stared right at me.

I swallowed hard and nodded. "Good evening, Mr. Bonner."

"Goodness me," Miz Beulah fussed. "I don't know where my manners got off to. This here is Mercy Kaplan, Monroe, the girl I told you about. She's come to help out till spring planting."

After a long moment, Mr. Bonner grunted and started in on his supper.

Embarrassment flitted across Miz Beulah's face, but she blinked it away, like she'd probably done her whole life long. She took the chair opposite him, leaving me no choice but to sit between them.

I hadn't eaten cornbread in a while, or soup with meaty salt pork, either, and I wasn't sure my stomach was up to it. It tasted real good, but it took a lot of small bites and sips of water to get it all down. I guess Miz Beulah remembered what it was like for her when she first got farmed out, because she gave my hand a sympathetic pat when Mr. Bonner wasn't looking. It did little to calm my insides, though.

When supper was finally done, I convinced Miz Beulah to sit in the parlor with Mr. Bonner for a spell while I cleaned up.

I figured washing dishes alone might give me a chance to sort out what it was he disliked about me.

I found it a wonder that someone like Miz Beulah could choose such a sour old soul to go through life with. She and Mr. Bonner were nothing alike. Smiles seemed to bubble from somewhere deep inside her, sweet and satisfying as springwater on a hot day, while he just sat there, hard and dry as an old bone. Whatever it was that brought them together had sure left her with the short end of the stick.

It finally came to me, though, that some terrible thing might've happened to make the old man such a disagreeable sort, but if so, Miz Beulah hadn't let on. She beamed her pleasure at me before she shuffled into the parlor, and the good feeling she left behind lasted me all through the dirty dishes.

I hung my cup towel on a hook to dry, started up the stairs to the attic, then stopped, dead still. I'd just heard Mama's voice, loud as thunder, fussing in my head.

Mercy, where are your manners, girl? she asked.

I cringed. The last thing I wanted to do was disturb that old man, but I turned around anyway and did what Mama would've expected.

I crept back across the kitchen floor and paused in the doorway for a moment, watching Mr. Bonner trying to read. He had on two pairs of glasses, one over the other, and held his book up close to the lamp that sat on the table between him and his wife. Miz Beulah sat crocheting, wrapping yarn around her crochet hook, moving it in and out of a big flower. More huge blooms of rose and pale pink lay crumpled in her lap, joined together like a patchwork quilt.

I stepped into the room and cleared my throat. Miz Beulah rested her arms and looked up, but Mr. Bonner kept on reading.

"I've finished the kitchen, Miz Beulah, and just wanted to say that, if there's nothing else, I'll go on to bed now."

"Thank you, Mercy. You do that. You've had a powerful long first day."

I felt an invisible nudge from Mama. "And I'd like to thank you, too, for your kind welcome," I added.

Mr. Bonner raised an eyebrow but never looked up.

"Well, it's us, Mercy Kaplan, who should be thanking you," she said. "Now, get yourself off to bed, and don't you worry one bit about when to get up. I'll just tap on the ceiling with my broom handle when it's time to make breakfast and do chores." She smiled. "Easier on my old knees."

I nodded and smiled back. With another quick glance at Mr. Bonner, I headed for the attic stairs. At least Miz Beulah liked me. That would be enough to get me through the months ahead. Yet, even before I reached my room, I wanted more. I guessed I'd have to give that old man some serious thought. Maybe there was a way to get him to like me, too.

I hadn't anticipated how dark the attic might be, and for a short while I just stood there at the top of the stairs, unwilling to cross the threshold. I focused on the dim circle of stars above my bed, then angled toward the chest, feeling for the lamp and the matches I'd seen there. With one strike, the match flared, and the welcome starlight disappeared in a flush of brightness, a last door slamming shut between me and home. A sharp pang for what I'd lost shuddered through me, but I tried to ignore the sick churning. I lit the lamp, peeled off my dress, and slipped between the fresh linens.

I was bone-tired, yet every time I closed my eyes I saw Mama, Papa, and the kids all over again, saying goodbye. I sucked in great swallows of musty air, determined not to cry, but the sorrow rolled down my cheeks anyway, and soaked right into my pillow.

chapter
6

THE NEXT DAY, Mr. Bonner came to breakfast wearing a nice shirt. "It's First Monday," Miz Beulah told me while we hurried to get biscuits on the table. "Mr. Bonner always takes the wagon into town for supplies on First Monday."

I knew all about that strange day. Papa took me with him into Canton once, right before spring planting, and I got to see all the exciting bartering that went on. He said it started long ago when a district judge decided to hold court in Canton's red brick courthouse on the first Monday of every month. People soon made a point of going to town on that day to do their trading and visit neighbors, and before long, the town square was full of horse traders and farmers peddling eggs, vegetables, and all kinds of tools. Even hunting dogs were bartered for on that day. With so much bickering and haggling taking place over those hounds, many took to calling it Dog Monday, but it didn't matter to me what they called it. It was an exciting day.

Mr. Bonner frowned while Miz Beulah went over the supply list with him, pointing out changes she'd made to their usual purchases. Seemed I'd be increasing the amount of goods they'd need, and I could tell he didn't care much for the extra expense. Being a burden didn't sit well with me, but at least Miz Beulah didn't see me that way.

We watched till the wagon disappeared over the rise, then whittled away at the chores that needed to be done before Mr. Bonner got back. Besides the usual cleaning and laundry, getting meals and feeding chickens, the cupboards had to be scrubbed and rearranged to make room for the new goods.

Only a glow was left on the horizon when Mr. Bonner returned that evening, and it was later still when we finally had all the provisions put away and sat down to supper. The Bonners were too tired for anything but bed that night. I was tired, too, though I figured the weight of my weariness lay in bending my will to please everyone but me. I fell asleep thinking I might never get used to this unfamiliar place.

Over the passing weeks, however, I finally found a rhythm to living with strangers. Though I didn't mention it, my seventeenth birthday came and went, reminding me that Mama had married Papa when she was just seventeen. It was hard to believe I was grown. I sure didn't feel any different. I flinched, thinking of how Charity would turn fifteen without me in a few months. I missed her terribly. I missed them all. Sometimes it felt like loneliness was all there was left of me.

Yet the long days with the Bonners did inch me closer to home, and with the eventual acceptance of my fate, Mama's lullabies came back to me. They filled my head while I worked, making the days more bearable somehow, and though my voice wasn't nearly as sweet as Mama's, I couldn't keep the songs from spilling out of me now and then.

One morning, after breakfast, while I scrubbed the kitchen sink, I saw Mr. Bonner through the window, listening to my singing. Right off, my cheeks flushed hot, but something in that old man's eyes kept me going despite my mortification.

For that brief moment, the hard lines on his face eased, as if he'd had a taste of summer melon or caught a whiff of blooming honeysuckle. I watched, curious, but when the lullaby was over, his expression shifted. His eyes grew dull, and he shuffled off to the barn to begin his day.

I wondered what it was in Mama's lullaby that had changed him so. I wondered, too, if this was the side of him that Miz Beulah had been drawn to from the start. Did she see it still, even though his eyes were often stony and his silence stung like north winds? I wasn't sure I could be that generous. But even as that stingy thought crept through me, I knew the tenderness I'd seen in that old man might help me tear down the fences between us. I knew, too, that I wouldn't rest till I'd found out what had made him the way he was.

"A small kindness now and then is better than manure," Mama told me once. "It can make the most surprising things grow."

I smiled, thinking of her. She'd been right about most things, even when I hadn't wanted her to be, so I summoned the pluck I needed and took to looking for little ways to please the old man.

I sang often after that, quietly, but always when Mr. Bonner was near, and he never failed to stop and listen. I put an extra strip of bacon on his breakfast plate and made sure the coffee was fresh when he came through the door every evening. I shined up his shoes, cleaned both pairs of reading glasses, and plumped the pillow he used after supper to ease his achy back. I never expected him to let on that he noticed, but in early November, after he made his monthly trip to town, I found a small bag of candy on my cot. I thanked Miz Beulah the next morning, figuring that the request had been on her list, but she shook her head.

"It weren't me," she said in breathy amazement. "I got one, too. I don't know what's gotten into that old man, but I sure ain't gonna do nothin' to disturb it."

That evening, Mr. Bonner came in from the fields and sat at the table with Miz Beulah, silent as usual. I wanted to thank him for the candy, but sometimes my words, no matter how few, appeared as welcome as a barn fire. When it came time to refill his coffee cup, I set it down in front of him and just stood there, all squirmy inside, till he finally looked up.

"Um, I just wanted to thank you, Mr. Bonner. For the sweets, I mean. It was very kind of you to think of me."

He grunted and pointed to my plate. "Better sit down. Your supper's gettin' cold."

Miz Beulah just smiled and kept on eating.

Later, when I was sweeping up the kitchen, I overheard Mr. Bonner in the parlor talking low, telling Miz Beulah about the news he'd heard in town. A new and terrible influenza was sweeping across Europe and Asia, infecting millions.

"It's spreadin' right through our troops fightin' the war over there," he said. "Newspapers are sayin' more soldiers have died from the dang disease than from battle wounds."

I set my broom aside and moved closer to the doorway.

"The sickness showed up in Kansas months ago," he went on, "and now it's croppin' up all over the country. Right here in Texas, too."

I heard Miz Beulah let out a breathy moan. "Is there anyone ailin' in town, Monroe?"

"Not yet, but folks are worried. They've heard tales of how it's all around us, how some towns have already closed their schools and businesses, and how even the churches ain't holdin' a single Sunday meetin' till it's over. The sickness peaks in two to three weeks. Does its killin', they say, then leaves as quick as it came. The federal health people are workin' on it, though, so maybe they'll slow it down 'fore it reaches us."

I thought of Papa, off somewhere working, or maybe still looking for work, and worry gnawed at me. I felt powerless. If only I knew where he was, whether he was safe.

I listened for more about the spreading sickness and was met by a stomach-churning silence. All I could do was pick up my broom and go back to my sweeping.

"Humanity has but three great enemies:
fever, famine and war; of these by far the greatest,
by far the most terrible, is fever."

SIR WILLIAM OSLER

chapter
7

I'D BEGUN TO THINK this was the warmest fall God ever made, but by mid-November, the weather finally cooled, making chores and sleeping a bit more agreeable. Mr. Bonner got some wonderful news from a passing neighbor about then, too. On November 11, an armistice had been signed by the Germans. The war was finally over, and our soldiers were leaving the trenches of France for good. Mr. Bonner told us all about it, right there in the kitchen.

I smiled, happy that the war had ended but relieved, too, that there'd been no more news about the influenza. Papa was safe and well. He had to be. Surely Mama would've gotten word to me by now if he wasn't.

Believing that helped me concentrate on work again. And crocheting. Miz Beulah had insisted I learn, and with my hands so busy, I didn't seem to worry about Papa as much.

"A body just needs to make something pretty now and then," she said, sitting me down with a ball of yarn and a cro-chet hook. "You'll know what I mean when the weather turns cold and there's nothing but bare trees and frosty brown grass to look at."

Soon I had flowers blooming in my lap, too, just like Miz Beulah.

After a while, I finally built up enough courage to ask her about her life, and we talked one evening while I peeled potatoes for supper. She didn't appear to mind telling me how she and Mr. Bonner met and married.

"That was about forty-five years ago, way back in the spring of 1873," she said.

After the wedding, she came to Canton with her new husband to live here on his daddy's farm. She even worked with him in the fields, and when the old man died, they took over the place as their own.

"Goodness me, we were young back then," she said. "And tough. We never once thought about gettin' old, and look at us now. Here we are with too much farm and not enough years or might left anymore to keep it going."

"None of your children want to take it on?" I asked.

For a brief moment, Miz Beulah's soft face folded in pain, and I glimpsed a wound so raw it scared me. I dropped the knife into my potato peelings, wiped my hands on my apron, and went to her.

"I'm . . . I'm sorry, Miz Beulah." I stood there, feeling helpless. "I didn't mean to pry."

She waved a hand at me and reached for the back of a kitchen chair. "It's nothin' to fret about, Mercy. Old sorrow has a way of sneakin' up on you sometimes, that's all. Rears its wretched head when you least expect it."

I helped her into the chair and fetched a glass of water.

"We had four children once," she said. "Three big boys and a baby girl. My oldest was barely twelve, but they've been gone a long time now."

"Here, Miz Beulah." I put the glass in her hands. "Take a sip of this, and don't think about all that sadness anymore."

"Oh, it's not all sad." She looked up at me. "Since you came, I've 'membered lots of good times. I think Mr. Bonner has, too, and thank goodness for it. I feared all that hate he carried around with him would follow him to his grave."

"Hate?"

She patted my hand. "Not for anyone else, Mercy. Just hisself."

"I don't understand."

"No, and I never did, neither. There weren't nothin' he coulda done to save 'em. Fever's got a mind of its own, it does. Picks and chooses. Lets some live on and takes others away. We weren't the only family who lost their little ones that winter."

I put my arm around her, remembering the fear I'd heard in her voice when Mr. Bonner told her about the new influenza spreading across the country. That terrible news must've ripped open old wounds, but it was *my* nosy questions that shot that unbearable grief right through her heart all over again.

Miz Beulah sighed and hauled herself up from her chair. "Mr. Bonner just never quite forgave hisself for livin' through it when none of our younguns did."

Trying to imagine what it was like having to bury every one of your children was like stepping up to the edge of a deep, dark well. I finally understood why Mr. Bonner was the way he was, but I had to back away from the misery I'd glimpsed. It was just so black and bottomless I couldn't make myself look any closer.

chapter
8

THANKSGIVING ROLLED AROUND, and I helped Miz Beulah make stuffing and sweet-potato pies. "But come Christmas, when the harvest is over and done, we'll have us a real party," she said. "We'll send Owen and Garrett to fetch your family."

Pleasure lit her round face. There probably wasn't much else in this world that would've made me happier, and Miz Beulah knew that. She put her arm around me and gave me a warm squeeze. "Yessiree, we're gonna have us a good time."

We sat down with the hired hands to a fine dinner of stuffed chicken, greens, and buttered biscuits. It was a wonderful meal, and with the promise of a Christmas visit from my family, I had an awful lot to be thankful for. Yet it was hard to eat and not think about the table at home. I couldn't help but worry about Mama and the kids.

When I brought out the sweet-potato pie, Owen grinned so wide I thought he'd bust a jawbone. The brothers were a funny pair, tall and lean, bucktoothed and freckled, but worrying about family didn't slow either of them down. They helped polish off that pie real quick, not wasting a crumb, and when Miz Beulah had me fetch the second one, they jumped up on either side of her and smacked her on the cheeks. She got all flustered, but it was the happiest I'd seen her. It wasn't hard to tell she loved those two young men like her own.

After dinner, Owen insisted that Miz Beulah sit in the parlor and relax with Mr. Bonner. "I can't recollect the last time me and Garrett sat down to a meal like that," he said. "It'd be our pure pleasure to help Mercy clean up."

I didn't know how I felt about having those two overgrown Denton boys helping me in the kitchen, but they got right to it, and the work was done lickety-split. They were soon sitting out on the porch with their feet propped up on the railing, appreciating their full bellies, no doubt, along with the last of their idle time before harvest.

With all the work out of the way, I went upstairs to dream about Christmas and home and to crochet another flower. Miz Beulah had given me all her yarn scraps, a bright palette of reds and blues, greens and yellows, enough for a small throw. I could already picture Mama sitting in her rocker, snuggled warmly beneath a field of colorful blooms. It would make a fine Christmas gift, and I could hardly wait to see her face when I gave it to her.

THE VERY NEXT DAY, Miz Beulah stepped off the porch wrong and twisted her ankle. I helped her into bed, and she fussed all the way.

"I ain't got time for this nonsense right now," she complained. "Those beets and cabbages ain't gonna wait on no

44

sprains. They're due at the packing house 'fore the end of next week."

"Those big men can take care of the harvest without you." I propped up her foot. "You need to just concentrate on getting better."

I bathed her ankle with cool water, but it still swelled something awful. "I'm afraid it might take a while for this to get better," I told her, "but don't you be worrying about a thing. I can handle the house and meals. And I can help Mr. Bonner, too, if he needs me." I gathered her Bible, her crochet, and my copy of *The Adventures of Tom Sawyer*, then left her so I could get started on chores.

When Mr. Bonner came through the door that evening, he took one look at the supper tray I'd made for Miz Beulah and headed straight for the bedroom. I heard him talking, soft and concerned, then he laughed, something I hadn't heard him do once since I'd arrived.

He walked back through the doorway with a smidgen of a smile still lingering at the corners of his mouth and picked up Miz Beulah's tray. "I'll be takin' my supper from a tray, too," he said, "if you don't mind fixin' one up for me."

"Yessir. I'll bring it in right away."

He nodded his thanks, and when he went back to the bedroom, I remembered what Mama told me about watching for heart signs. It struck me that Mr. Bonner wasn't much different from the candy he'd brought from town—hard on the outside and soft on the inside. His thoughtfulness in giving us sweets had said a lot about him, but seeing the tenderness he had for Miz Beulah was the true signpost for me. I was beginning to like this old man.

I ran upstairs, grabbed the last two pieces of candy from my bag, and placed them on his tray. Miz Beulah grinned when she saw the sweets and reached for Mr. Bonner's hand.

"She's a good one, Monroe. I'd sure keep her if we only could."

He pushed a fork into her hand, ignoring her remark, but the glitter in his eyes told me I'd finally gotten what I wanted. The old man liked me, too.

I managed to keep up with the additional chores over the next few days, but it was Mr. Bonner who tended Miz Beulah through the nights. He carried in her supper trays and straightened her sheets and pillows, and each evening, as I went up to bed, I'd hear her reading snippets of Tom Sawyer's adventures out loud to him. Her voice followed me up the stairs and into the attic, and though I could never quite make out the words from my cot, I took comfort in the soft murmurings. They floated up from below, reminding me of the way Mama and Papa talked once we kids had settled in for the night. And, without fail, I'd drift right off.

chapter 9

MIZ BEULAH WASN'T HEALING as fast as I'd thought she would. I suspected the fall might've done a little more than twist her ankle and asked if we shouldn't get the doctor out to look her over. She waved her hands in the air to shush me.

"Don't go talkin' like that, Mercy. Mr. Bonner don't need nothin' gettin' in the way of that harvest. He'll be takin' the first loaded wagon in to George Hilliard at the mercantile to trade for supplies tomorrow. If he puts it off, we'll be the ones eatin' all those beets and cabbages, and we won't even have cornbread to go with 'em."

I nodded. I'd already noticed that many things wouldn't last out the week. "We're almost out of coffee now," I told her.

"See? And you sure don't wanna be around Mr. Bonner when he don't get his coffee."

That night, when I brought them their supper trays, Miz Beulah was trying to reason with him.

"But, Monroe," she said, "I've got Mercy. We'll do fine while you're away."

He shook his head. "This first load is going straight to George. I'll just send Owen. He can handle it."

Miz Beulah shot me an exasperated look. "Well, you better bring me that supply list, Mercy. If I don't make clear ever' little thing, that boy's liable to read 'flour' and bring home daisies."

I laughed and fetched the list.

Early the next morning the men added tall sideboards to the wagon and loaded it high with beets and cabbages. When Owen left for town, I turned to the monthly chore of cleaning and organizing the cupboards. With so much to do, the day flew by, but well before sunset, I saw Owen coming back down the road. He was early. I went out to help him bring in the supplies, but he shook his head.

"No need a-worrying yourself with this. You go on in and keep Miz Beulah company. Me and Garrett'll put away all this stuff for you."

He looked a little strange, but I couldn't put a finger on why. "Are you feeling poorly, Owen?" I asked finally. "Or maybe just hungry? I'd be happy to get you a little something before you start unloading the wagon."

He shook his head again. "Thank you, but I'm right as rain. You just stop frettin' and go on inside. Tell Miz Beulah that George Hilliard at the store said he got everything she wanted."

I nodded and headed back to the kitchen, but before I got in, I overheard Owen talking to Garrett and Mr. Bonner.

"It's bad," Owen said. "They're calling it Spanish influenza."

I stepped inside but stayed near the screen door.

"People been sick and dying for almost three weeks now, Mr. Bonner. Mr. Hilliard wouldn't even let me in his store. He said I'd have to unload the cabbages into a bin out back, and that the only way he'd fill my order was if I slid the list under the door."

I peeked out the kitchen window. Garrett stood rooted to the ground, staring at his brother like he'd sprouted a second pair of ears. Mr. Bonner leaned heavily against the wagon; his head hung low. "How many?" he asked.

Owen looked confused. "Sir?"

Mr. Bonner raised his head, and with a patience that surprised me, he asked again, his words calm and slowly paced, "Did George say how many have died, Owen?"

"No, sir, but I reckon it's a powerful number. I saw caskets stacked up like cordwood, and a wagon sittin' 'twixt Hilliard's and the Palace Drug Store all covered up. Doc Kellam was worryin' over it. I can't say for sure, but iffin' I was a bettin' man, I'd wager it was loaded with dead folks."

Mr. Bonner nodded. "Well, I guess there ain't much we can do about it now. You boys get the provisions in, and I'll get Mercy to fix you up a big pan of that stew she's been working on so's you can get to bed early. Tomorrow I wanna start out before daylight. We should be able to get two loads to the packing house by dark."

I turned from the window, weighed down with all I'd heard. I'd been to town with Papa only once, and though I didn't know any of the people there, I found myself remembering faces, wondering if this one or that one had taken ill. I refused even to consider that Papa might be in danger. Surely he was clean away from all this sickness by now. Mama and the kids had to be okay, too, living out so far and having no money to take them into town. Maybe being poor had its rewards after all. I said a quick prayer of thanks, trying to hang on to that probability, but the nagging doubt never quite went away. I could feel it squirming inside me, like a busy spider weaving a deadly web.

I ladled up a big pan of stew for the boys and went in to give Owen's message to Miz Beulah, but I couldn't bring myself to tell her what I'd overheard. I didn't want to see that long-ago pain darken her face again. Besides, the bad news would surely be easier to take if it came from Mr. Bonner.

Supper was over early, and once the dishes were washed and put away, I noticed the dreadful quiet. It slithered through the rooms, exposing every creak and sigh as the house's old bones settled in for the night. I felt it reach for me, too, stealing into my head, threatening to reveal each flaw, each crack in my hopes for Papa.

I shuddered, refusing to feed my fears, and blew out the lamps. Mr. Bonner must've already told Miz Beulah the news by now. I stood there in the moon's blue light, thinking of how her poor heart must be aching for all the sick little ones out there.

While climbing the dark stairway, I longed for the soft murmurings that had drifted up from the Bonners' bedroom during the past evenings, but *Tom Sawyer* had no doubt been put aside. On this worrisome night, we'd all have to find a way to fall asleep on our own.

chapter
10

BEFORE DAYLIGHT the next day, Mr. Bonner sent Owen to the packing house with the second loaded wagon while he and Garrett harvested more cabbage for the third trip. I looked in on Miz Beulah often and never once caught her reading or crocheting. She'd hardly touched her breakfast, either. It was clear she'd been fretting over the sickness in town. I decided a sweet bread pudding to go with supper might please her, so I gathered up some fresh eggs and milk and got started.

Around midday, I saw Owen coming back from town. He lingered on the empty wagon seat for a moment, his head in his hands, then slowly climbed down. When I looked again, the wagon had been reloaded, but Owen was nowhere in sight. Garrett was the one headed to town this time. It surprised me. Mr. Bonner always seemed to put a lion's share of trust in Owen, but with so much to do, maybe the men had decided to trade off.

I grabbed a cup towel and pulled my surprise dessert from the oven. It smelled sweet and tempting. I hoped it would lift Miz Beulah's spirits, but when the work was done and Mr. Bonner joined her for supper, *he* was the one who made her smile.

"Bread puddin' is a favorite of his," Miz Beulah said.

I watched him take a bite, slowly nod, then plunge his spoon back into the bowl.

She laughed. "You must've done a mighty good job, Mercy. He's gonna polish that off and send you to the kitchen for more, mark my words."

He gave me a sideways look, just long enough for a wink. Satisfaction welled inside me. It felt good to see the two of them smile.

Later that night, a loud banging slipped between me and my dreams. I jolted awake. My first thought was that Miz Beulah must've tried to get up and fallen. I jumped to my feet and ran down the attic stairs in my nightgown, but it wasn't her at all.

The banging came again, louder and more insistent. Someone was at the kitchen door.

"Mr. Bonner!" a voice called.

It sounded like Owen. I lit the lamp, grabbed Miz Beulah's shawl from its hook, and threw open the door.

But it wasn't Owen. It was Garrett standing in front of me, eyes wide and fearful.

"I need help," he blurted out.

Mr. Bonner stepped through the kitchen doorway, smoothing his ruffled gray hair. "What's all the noise about?"

"Owen's terrible sick, Mr. Bonner, and I don't know what to do for him."

"I'll go," I said, headed for the door, but with one glance at Mr. Bonner, I stopped dead still.

He glared at me and shook his head. "I don't want you leaving this house, Mercy. You hear?"

I stared at him, surprised at the sternness in his voice.

"You stay right here and take care of Mrs. Bonner." He left, pulling the door shut behind him.

I slid the shawl from my shoulders and hung it back on the hook. Thoughts of how the influenza had swept through town troubled me. Owen had been there just yesterday. Though he hadn't been allowed in the store, he'd been right there, where that terrible sickness hung in the air like death itself, hovering over streets, beating its black wings against windows and doors.

I shuddered at the sinister image and went upstairs to dress. Daybreak was still more than an hour away, but I wanted to make sure Mr. Bonner had coffee when he came back in. I thought about taking it out to him, but after the determined way he'd made his wishes known, I decided I'd better wait. I'd just get a pot going on the stove, fry up some bacon, and put some biscuits in the oven.

I hurried back downstairs and looked in on Miz Beulah. Her lamp was out, but instead of the soft, steady breathing that sleep brings, I heard only the thick silence of worry. I tiptoed past her door, hesitant to disturb her, and headed to the kitchen.

A bright glow sat on the horizon by the time Mr. Bonner came back in. He quietly closed the door and just stood there while I poured him a cup of coffee and set it on the table.

For a long moment he didn't move at all. I waited, and when he finally glanced up at me, I saw a look so haunted I couldn't bring myself to ask about Owen. I pulled out a chair instead, and hurried to him.

"Please, Mr. Bonner, come sit down. I made some coffee. You take a sip of that and you'll feel better right away."

He let me lead him to the table, and I eased into the seat across from him, unsure of what to say or do. No one had volunteered to tell me about the sickness in town. I guess they wanted to spare me the worry, but surely Mr. Bonner would tell me now, with Owen so bad off. If I could only get him to talking.

"I've got bacon and biscuits ready," I told him. "And I'd be happy to fry you some eggs to go with it. I could fix up some for Owen and Garrett, too."

His eyes flashed pure fire. "Didn't I tell you to stay away from them boys?"

I flinched from the sudden lashing and stared at him, stunned.

"Didn't I?" he demanded again.

Still stinging from his sharp words, I nodded and grappled for a way to reassure him. "Yes, Mr. Bonner. I'll stay right here if that's what you want, but, please, you have to tell me about Owen. He's okay, isn't he?"

Mr. Bonner let out a slow breath and leaned heavily against the table.

"He's dead," he whispered. "The boy's dead."

chapter
II

OWEN DEAD? It couldn't be possible! He'd been loading the wagon just yesterday, working alongside Mr. Bonner and Garrett, preparing for his second trip to town. How could he have sickened and died so quickly?

Mr. Bonner stared into his cup. I could tell he was suffering. Seeing such unrelenting pain in his eyes had been almost more than I could bear. I ached to put my arms around him, tell him it would be okay, but I knew, for him, nothing would be okay again. Those young men meant far more to him than just hired hands. They'd become the boys fever stole from him years ago. They'd become his own.

He gulped down his coffee, pushed himself up from the table, and headed to the bedroom. I cringed at the thought of poor Miz Beulah hearing the awful news and wished I could take this burden from her. It seemed to me that life had already dealt her more than her generous heart should have to endure.

With dread I watched Mr. Bonner disappear through the doorway, and after a short moment, I heard the crying. I'd expected it, but I hadn't foreseen what it would do to me. The pitiful sound of Miz Beulah's anguish cut right through me, sharp and deep, till tears rolled down my cheeks, too. I wiped them away, but I couldn't break free of the terrible fear they'd left behind. Whatever would I do if I lost Papa? Or Mama? Or one of the kids?

With no warning, I fell into the black hole my life would become if influenza took even one of them away, and suddenly there was no air. I couldn't breathe. "Oh, Miz Beulah," I whispered, choking back new tears. "You lost all four of your children. How did you ever go on?"

When Miz Beulah's sobs settled, Mr. Bonner went outside to take the sideboards off the wagon. Clearly there'd be no trips to town today. Garrett would need to take his brother home to be buried.

Before long, I saw the two men carrying Owen's blanket-wrapped body to the wagon bed. I peered through the window at Garrett. He looked terrible. The dreadful pain of losing a brother had taken its toll, but I feared that wasn't all that had him looking so done in. He'd been to town, too, just like Owen, and though I didn't want to consider it, that terrible sickness could already have a hold on him, too.

The men eased Owen into the wagon, then stood there like they couldn't bring themselves to say their goodbyes. Mr. Bonner plucked some bills and coins from his pocket and stuffed them into Garrett's hand. "It's not enough," he said, "but it's everything we got from the two loads of cabbage yesterday."

Garrett stared at his feet. "Thank you, Mr. Bonner. I'll be back tomorrow evening, for sure, and we'll finish the harvest."

Mr. Bonner nodded. "You just take care of your brother. We'll get by till then."

Garrett climbed into the wagon and headed west.

By noon, the sky had turned dark and broody, but Mr. Bonner said Garrett was probably home by then. A steady rain soon had us bottled up in the house, making a pitiful threesome of us the rest of that day. I kept up with chores and made more bread pudding, though none of us felt much like eating.

Miz Beulah had begun to hobble around, which pleased Mr. Bonner, but it hardly seemed worth her effort. She never appeared satisfied, no matter where she sat, and continued to move from place to place, searching for comfort that a feather pillow or cushion could never give her. That kind of solace had been whisked away with Owen, and it'd probably be a long time before she found it again.

The sky turned fair by midmorning the second day, and we sat late into the evening, watching for Garrett till it was clear he wouldn't be coming.

"He'll be here tomorrow," Miz Beulah said with certainty. "First thing, I'm betting."

Mr. Bonner nodded slowly.

But Garrett didn't come back the next morning, or that evening, either, and by nightfall of the third day, Mr. Bonner looked far more drained than usual. I couldn't help but recall how Owen had dragged himself from the wagon after that second trip to town, like he was almost too worn out to walk. He must've been sick even then. And Garrett had that same haggard look when he left us the next morning.

Worry clouded Miz Beulah's face, and now I was worried, too. If the sickness took Owen that fast, then Garrett might already be gone.

I tried to get Mr. Bonner to lie down, fearful of the growing weariness I saw in him, but he wouldn't budge. He remained in the parlor till he was sure Garrett wasn't coming.

When he finally gave up and went to bed, Miz Beulah insisted I get some rest, too, but with Mr. Bonner looking so poorly, I hesitated. I couldn't go till I'd coaxed a promise from her to holler if she needed anything. With a nod and a swish of her hand, she shooed me to the attic.

Upstairs, a sudden wind raked against the siding, and rain returned to pepper the circle window. Shivering, I slipped out of my dress, pulled my gown over my head, and slid under the covers.

I said my prayers, hoping to quiet the awful fear that lurked inside me, but I knew sleep wouldn't come easy this night. My head was too full. Owen had said the whole world was suffering, which made me wonder how many people might be praying for loved ones right this very minute. If Owen was right, God must be flooded with millions of voices. I added my own, but I didn't see how He could possibly hear another prayer.

Long before daybreak, the rain stopped. I soon smelled

coffee and bacon and crept downstairs to find Miz Beulah, hands folded in her lap, waiting at the kitchen table. An envelope lay in front of her. She looked up at me with her jaw clenched, eyes stern, the same way Mr. Bonner had looked when he first heard that Owen was ailing.

Fear prickled through me. "Are you okay, Miz Beulah?" I asked.

She nodded, but I could tell she wasn't. "You're not sick, are you?"

"I'm fine, Mercy. I'm fine." She ran a hand over the edge of the tablecloth, smoothing imaginary wrinkles, and without looking up, she said, "Mr. Bonner's got the fever."

My heart skipped and thudded hard. It was what I'd feared most, but I just stood there, staring at her. I didn't want to accept what this might mean.

"But people get sick all the time," I argued. "It's probably nothing at all to worry about." I took a plate from the cupboard and turned to the stove. "I'll fix up a tray for Mr. Bonner and feed him myself. He'll take some food from me, you'll see, and he'll be better in no time."

Miz Beulah snatched the plate from my hand and shoved it back on the shelf. "You'll do no such thing." She pushed me into a chair. "I don't want you anywhere near that bedroom, you hear? And he don't, neither."

I'd never seen such raw determination in her eyes. She hobbled to the cupboard and pulled out a coffee tin. Coins rattled onto the table.

"It's not much, just a dollar and twenty-two cents, but with the crop still in the fields, that's all there is right now."

Confusion tumbled in my head. "But Garrett will be here soon and—"

"He's not coming back," she said. "He would've been here already if he could've."

Her voice sounded distant and indifferent, though I knew she couldn't possibly feel that way. I searched her face for some sign of emotion, but there wasn't a single tear in her eyes, not even a hint of the crushing weight that had to lie behind her words. I saw only a dogged resolve.

"You gotta go, Mercy. Right now," she said.

Now? Shock erupted inside me. I couldn't leave now! She needed me. I cocked my head in disbelief and watched as she raked the coins off the table, picked up the envelope, and pushed it all into my hands. "Take this money, and this letter telling about your good work here, and go home to your mama."

Go home? I felt a brief flutter of anticipation, then shoved it aside. "But . . . but, Miz Beulah, I can't leave. With Garrett gone, who's gonna milk the cow? And what if you get sick, too? There'll be no one here to look after either one of you."

"I milked cows long before you were born, Mercy Kaplan, and I ain't sick. Don't intend to be, neither. I can take care of Mr. Bonner on my own."

"But—"

"Not another word. You'll do as you're told, you hear?"

I shook my head again, hard this time. "I have to see Mr. Bonner," I told her.

I headed to the bedroom, but she grabbed my arm and swung me around not two steps from his door. "He wants you gone," she whispered, "and you'll *not* go against his wishes."

She glared at me with fierce determination, while the sound of Mr. Bonner's labored breathing rattled from the dark room, rattled right through every part of me.

I finally hung my head, and tears dripped from the end of my nose and onto the wood floor. "I just can't leave like this, Miz Beulah. Please don't ask me to."

She loosened her grip on my arm. "You surely can, Mercy, and you will. There ain't no way I'm gonna lose another child to fever. Now, get up to that attic and get your things." Her voice softened. "I'll pack the bacon I fried up for you, and some of that good bread you made yesterday, so you won't go hungry on the road."

I wanted to shout at her, tell her I wouldn't leave, but the look in her eyes drained away my will.

She waited, blocking the door to Mr. Bonner's bedroom, till I had no choice but to go upstairs and pack.

"When sorrows come, they come not single spies
But in battalions."

WILLIAM SHAKESPEARE, *HAMLET*

chapter 12

OUTSIDE, NORTH WINDS bit at my cheeks and gusted around my legs while the sound of Mr. Bonner's grim struggle for breath haunted me. I stared at the house with its one dim light shining from the kitchen window, stunned that I stood at road's edge once again with my belongings in a flour sack.

I didn't know what to do. I couldn't bring myself to leave, and yet Miz Beulah wouldn't let me stay. What would happen if she caught the fever, too?

I squeezed my eyes shut, trying to block out the sudden picture of the two of them lying dead in their bed, then finally gave my head a hard shake. No, it couldn't happen. It just couldn't. Miz Beulah looked fine. She and Mr. Bonner had survived the fever years ago, even when their little ones were dying all around them. They'd survive this, too. They had to.

Hesitant to leave them, I finally turned my feet toward home, but with every step down the road I felt the Bonners tugging at me, pulling me back. That old couple had made me one of their own, and somehow, I'd done the same with them. I just hadn't realized how much they'd come to mean to me till now. They took me in, gave me a place to sleep, and sat me at their table, right there beside them, when Mama and Papa couldn't. They protected me, first from the worry, then from the sickness, and though I'd done as they insisted, I knew a part of me would stay behind, wishing to give them the daughter that fever had stolen away so long ago.

My foot slipped, forcing me to rip my thoughts from the Bonners and watch my step. Heavy rains had turned the road into a river of mud that clung to my shoes and splattered my stockings. I stuck to the higher ground between the ruts, picking my way, and managed to stay reasonably dry, but each step away from the Bonners beat in my chest like a drum of worry.

I hugged Miz Beulah's old coat tighter around me. She'd insisted that I take it, just before she shoved me out the door. One pocket jingled with coins, and the other bulged slightly with the folded envelope.

I tried to push my thoughts toward home, and when I could finally think of Mama and the kids again, my step lightened and my pace quickened. I wanted to feel Mama's arms around me and hear the latest news from Papa. I wanted to dodge Honor's slobbery kisses, rough up Justice's curls, and listen to Charity carry on and on about *Jane Eyre*—or anything. It didn't matter what, as long as I was back home. I smiled. They'd all be surprised when they saw me.

With the road so muddy, I knew today's walk would probably take longer than before, so I spent the extra hours letting memory walk me through our old weathered cabin. I heard again the creak of Mama's rocker and smelled her rabbit stew simmering on the stove. I helped Justice learn his letters and played peek-a-boo with Honor. I snuggled under my warm quilt and watched lamplight flickering across rafters. Nothing escaped my attention.

I wallowed in those memories, and more, for a good while. Sure, I still wanted to leave home one day, wanted to make a different kind of life for myself, but over the last few months I'd discovered a sweetness in everyday things I'd never noticed before. I guess living without Mama, Papa, and the kids had brought that home to me better than anything could.

My flour sack bumped against my leg, making me think of Christmas. The mud-splattered bag bulged with eight big crocheted flowers, already joined together, and enough yarn for another four. Miz Beulah said I had a fast hand and a good eye for this kind of work. It wouldn't be long before Mama's Christmas throw would be finished. Just the thought of Mama's face on Christmas morning set off a flurry of expectation inside me. I couldn't wait to see her sitting in her rocker, covered with my bright flowers. She'd be toasty warm. And proud. And I'd feel . . . well, I'd just feel happy.

Before I knew it, I'd passed the tree where I'd had my noon meal months ago. I didn't stop this time, though. I was too impatient. I pulled out my bacon and bread and ate while I walked.

By late evening, I finally saw the Gurtry farm and glanced

skyward, recalling the way smoke from our chimney used to look curling against the vast blue. I'd see it again soon.

I picked up my pace once more, measuring the time it used to take me to get home from the Gurtrys' fields. When I spotted the footpath to our cabin, my heart skipped. I rounded the bend and finally caught my first glimpse of home, hushed against a background of brown grass and dark clouds tinged pink and gold.

I slowed, uneasy, staring at the unspoiled grounds. Something wasn't right. Justice's footprints should've been everywhere. Surely he would've tracked mud all over the steps by this late hour. I squinted above the cabin to the breathless chimney, and my uneasiness turned into fear.

I ran, no longer careful of the slushy holes in the path. Mud flew from my shoes, splashing my dress and leaving dark splatters across the brown grass.

"Mama!" I called. "Charity!"

I tugged my wet skirt from my legs, struggled up the steps, and threw open the unlocked door.

My ears rang with the sudden silence. From the doorway, I quickly scanned the cabin, from Mama's rocking chair to the loft to the black stove standing dusty and cold in the kitchen. My muddy flour sack slid from my fingers, slapping the rough pine floor with a sound that echoed around the walls and knifed right through me.

No one was here.

Disappointment sucked the air right out of me. The cabin

looked as if Mama and the kids had been gone for a while. But where could they be?

Papa—maybe he came home, maybe they all had to leave. But surely they wouldn't have left without coming to get me first.

The squirming doubt I'd carried for Papa reared up, grasping at Mama and the kids, threatening to tangle them all in its black web.

But no. Word would've gotten back to me. Wouldn't it?

It had to be something else. I turned to look behind me, staring down the path till dampness shivered up my spine. Of course. The Gurtrys. They had to be at the Gurtrys'.

I grabbed my things, jerked around to leave, then stopped. The setting sun had already disappeared behind more black clouds. I stared toward the dusky road and the promise of more rain, and finally let my flour sack fall to the floor again. I'd waited this long. I could wait till morning.

I remembered old Tucker and went out back to check on him. He was gone, probably with Mama and the kids. Or maybe sold.

I gathered some kindling and firewood, but it wasn't till I had a fire crackling behind the stone hearth that I saw a folded paper on the mantel. A note from Mama? I grabbed it up and read the hurried scrawl.

Four Kaplan bodies buried this day,
November 16, 1918.

The words ripped through me, razor-sharp.

Female, mid-thirties.
Female, mid-teens.
Male, four-five years.
Female, one year.

No! It wasn't true! I stared at the words, then shook my head hard. It just wasn't! It was a trick, that's what it was.

An angry heat leaped inside me. How could anyone play such a hideously cruel joke? I turned the paper over—it was blank—then flipped it back and read the list again.

Mama and Charity?

Justice and Honor?

My hands shook, and the paper rattled.

All of them?

Horror crashed inside me and rumbled right through to my bones. I fell headlong into the bottomless black hole I'd only glimpsed with Miz Beulah's loss. I couldn't see. I couldn't move. I struggled through the darkness and forced myself to read the date again. November 16. Just three weeks ago?

I opened the back door and stood at the edge of the yard, searching for disturbances in the soil, but I saw none. I squinted toward the big oak growing on the rise. If my family were truly gone, that's where they'd probably be.

Dread trembled through me. I made my way across the spongy wet ground, and there, beneath the tree's stark limbs,

I found them. Four graves, rain-melted and bare of grass. I stared, numb.

I saw no markers, but I didn't need them. Mama lay beside her babies. Justice's and Honor's tiny graves were on her right, and Charity was on her left.

The agonizing truth slammed into me, bending me double, beating me down till I could deny it no longer.

It was true.

God, please help me, it was true!

I fell to my knees, and I cried.

chapter 13

THE NIGHT went on and on. I lay curled in front of the dying fire, tossing in brief moments of tormented sleep, only to be awakened by my own sobs.

The sun finally rose, splashing streaks of pale winter light across the floor, but it held no warm promise for me. My heart had already turned cold. My blood had thickened and hardened in my veins. I lay there, unable to move, unable to reason, letting the day creep over me.

When the light finally faded and slipped away, I pulled my pallet around me and slid into forgetfulness.

DON'T BE FOOLISH, GIRL; GET GOING!

The words bolted through my restless sleep and left me dangling in disbelief.

"Mama?" I called.

I peered through the bleary morning, hope thumping wild in my chest. It was her; I was sure of it. I'd heard her clear as day!

I jumped from my pallet by the fireplace and ran to the back porch, Mama's voice still ringing in my head. I couldn't have been mistaken. She *had* to be here.

I searched all the way to the oak, then stood there in my thin dress and bare feet, staring at the graves in the cold and damp till my fiery burst of hope burned away.

There'd been no voice.

I must've been dreaming.

Tears stung, and, like last night, sobs dropped me to my knees. I buried my wet face in my hands, and a blazing pain engulfed me, swallowing me whole.

"Mama," I moaned.

I gulped air, swiped at my wet cheeks, and peered up at the pale dawn sky. "I don't care if Justice wipes his dirty mouth on a hundred shirts. I'll wash them all. Every one! Please, just bring them back. Let all this be a horrible mistake."

Chill winds whistled around my ears.

I waited. Listening, hoping, imploring.

God was silent.

From nowhere, anger rushed in, pounding in my head, clenching my fists. "Why aren't You listening?" I shouted at the heavens. "You should've taken *me*, not the babies! And Charity's the one who had dreams and talent for better, not me!"

I wrapped my arms around my belly and sobbed. I ached. I ached so bad I wished I'd die.

"All I've had is contempt for my lot in life and a greedy desire for more," I whispered. "What kind of God rewards that?"

Wind billowed my dress. I shivered hard, and the last of my sudden defiance trickled right out of me, leaving me weak and empty.

"What am I supposed to do without them?" I pleaded. "Where am I supposed to go now?"

Again I waited for a sign, some small acknowledgment that this wrong could be righted. Crows fluttered high in bare branches, wind rustled brown leaves and winter grasses, and still there was nothing.

I finally pushed myself up, my body stiff and heavy, and I stared down at the four graves. "Please don't leave me, Mama," I whispered. "I need you. I don't know what to do."

Once more I waited, but there were no answers, not from God and not from Mama.

Reality sank inside me like a stone, cold and hard. I'd never again feel Mama's protective arms around me, or hear Honor and Justice giggle while they played, or curl up in the loft beside Charity, listening to her stories in the dark. They were gone. God had taken them all. And He'd left me nothing.

Again anger circled. I could feel its dark poison oozing back into my heart all over again. I spun around and strode toward the cabin. I could not, *would* not waste another minute on this foolish self-pity. Clearly no one could help me now. I was on my own, and, dream or no dream, I'd gotten at least one unmistakable message: I couldn't stay here.

My stomach rumbled as I made my way back to the cabin, and though it was from a hunger I had no desire to feed, the emptiness had left me queasy. I'd have to eat, and then I'd have to figure out what to do next.

I cleaned the mud from my feet, sat down on my pallet, and

fished the scraps of bread that I hadn't finished Saturday from my flour sack. I choked down the few bites and realized there was really only one thing I could do. If Papa was still alive, I had to find him. And my only chance to make that happen lay in town.

I washed my face, combed and braided my hair, then pulled Miz Beulah's folded envelope from my pocket. She'd written a simple note, praising my good nature and abilities to anyone interested in hiring me. Her parting gift made me long for her reassuring comfort all over again, and for a moment I let myself consider the notion of going back to her. She'd be cross, but only at first. She'd understand when I told her what had happened. She'd put her arms around me and soothe away this nightmare so I could breathe again.

I stared out the window, past the graves, and right into Miz Beulah's kitchen. Hope sparked, guttered, then died. With a defeated sigh, I returned the letter to my pocket. She'd made her wishes clear. I couldn't go back. And I couldn't stay here, either.

I looked around the cabin and saw Mama's delicate china cups still sitting on the mantel. It hurt even to think of leaving them, but I didn't know where I'd end up, and I couldn't bear the thought of breaking them. I left a message for Mr. Gurtry instead, asking him to keep them safe for me. I placed my note on the mantel, next to the first, then climbed up to the loft.

There I saw Justice's arrowhead and tin soldier, and a new burst of loss caught me unawares. In a blur of tears, I stared at the rough plank floor by his shelf. He'd played right there the morning I left.

I reached for the toys. "I'll take good care of them for you," I whispered.

Charity's tablets and diary were there on her shelf, too, just as I'd last seen them. I thumbed through the pages, longing to see a small glimpse of her flowing script again, but I was afraid to read even a single word, afraid that hearing her voice in my head might raze what was left of my courage.

With a last look around the loft, I hugged everything to my chest, climbed back down, and went to get Mama's unfinished throw from my flour sack. I'd have to leave it to make room for Justice's toys and Charity's stories. I draped the crocheted flowers across the back of the rocker, setting it in motion, and the soft, familiar creak of runners against floor made my eyes well up again. I'd never have a chance to give her my gift now, never get to see her proud smile.

I brushed at my wet cheeks, grabbed my mud-stained flour sack, and stuffed the kids' things inside. Without a single look back, I stepped onto the porch, trying hard not to think about how I was leaving Mama and Charity, Justice and Honor lying cold in the ground. I tugged the door closed, listening for the click, imagining the sound echoing off walls, the fireplace, Mama's stove, ringing hollow like the emptiness inside me. I squeezed my eyes shut till the only sound left was the wind, then turned toward the road. I had to find Papa. Beyond that, nothing else mattered anymore.

I headed off toward Canton, anxious to get to the post office. The walk into town was shorter than the one to the Bonners'. It wouldn't take quite as long, but with the roads so muddy and the weather so fickle, there was no way to know for sure. There'd been rain off and on for days now, but, wet or dry, I'd get to town. I had to.

I put one foot in front of the other and tried to think about watching for the good that might be coming, like Mama told me to do so long ago. It was hard, though, when I felt so dead inside.

I'd been keeping an eye on the gathering clouds, willing them to go away, and 'long about midday I heard a sputtering rumble behind me. With all the walking I'd done these last two days, I hadn't seen another soul on the road. Now a mud-spattered truck was headed straight toward me.

I stepped aside to let it pass, but it coughed gray smoke and slowed, squishing to a stop beside me. I grimaced at the smell of hot oil and gasoline and squinted through the window at the young man driving.

He leaned over and looked at me. "You shouldn't oughta be out on the road today, miss. Ain't you seen the weather coming?"

I nodded. "But I've got to get to town."

"Well, get in, then, 'fore the rain hits again, and I'll take you."

He drew a small stack of boxes up tight beside him, reached across to pull the handle, and shoved the door open. "I'm Josh Logan."

Nodding again, I told him my name and peered inside the cab, staring at the steering wheel, the pedals, the gauges, feeling a bit nervous at the thought of riding in something that didn't have a horse or mule strapped to it.

"Whatcha doin' way out here all alone?" he asked, running a handkerchief over the torn leather seat.

"I need to find work, but mostly I need to find my papa." I glanced toward home. In another minute I might be speeding away from Mama and the kids, and I wasn't so sure that was a good thing. Just walking down this road one step at a time seemed more than my heart could manage. One look at the deepening clouds, however, and I could almost hear Mama fussing at me, telling me how foolish I was, trying to hang on to what was already gone. Strange how just thinking of her made me feel less alone, like maybe a part of her was right there with me. It was a welcome solace. I surrendered, climbed into the truck, and settled myself on the vibrating seat.

"I ain't been back home long enough to know who might be hiring," he said. "Just long enough to see that things been topsy-turvy for weeks now, what with the epidemic and all. I been thankin' the good Lord ever' day that it appears to've moved on."

"Moved on?" The rumbling engine made the words tingle off the tip of my tongue.

"Yes'm. Looks like it done its worst, at least in Canton, and finally let us be so we could bury our dead." He gave me a sideways glance. "I lost a brother and a father three weeks ago."

Pain creased his forehead, and his eyes narrowed, like the loss was still too raw to speak of. He pulled in an uneven breath and asked, "How'd you and yours come out?"

I didn't want to tell him. Saying it out loud would make it real, but then it *was* real. Nothing could change that now.

"I lost my mama," I whispered finally, and felt my eyes sting. "My brother and two sisters, too." I blinked hard, trying to hold back the tears.

He flinched and shook his head. "Real sorry to hear that, miss. Sometimes it feels like the whole world has lost somebody. Doc Kellam said the sickness moved faster than anythin' he ever did see. But, you know, the town's shakin' it off now. There ain't been no new cases in Canton for four days, and that's a real good sign." He patted the boxes between us. "Mr. Cole, the pharmacist at the Palace Drug Store, sent me for this here medicine, but I doubt he'll need it now."

I nodded, relieved to hear some good news.

"So where you goin' in town?"

I made a quick decision. "Doc Kellam's," I told him. "The doc's office will do just fine."

I wanted to tell the doctor about Mr. Bonner, and it wouldn't hurt to ask him about Garrett and his family, too. He might know something. Then I'd go straight to the post office to see if Papa had sent a letter.

I slid my arms around my flour sack and leaned back, my new choices skipping through me like stones across water. I was grateful to have some kind of plan, no matter how small, but it was a shallow relief. The hurt was a great sea, far too deep and vast to be soothed by anything other than news of Papa.

Fat raindrops hit the windshield, making me jump with surprise. I'd been lucky to escape a cold soaking, and at this speed, I'd be in Canton very soon. Yet worry about finding work simmered inside me. All I knew how to do was cook, clean, and look after kids. Funny that, after all those nights lying awake, trying to imagine what big promise the world held for me, I never once pictured myself doing more of what I'd always done. I thought it would be something new and exciting. At this point, however, I was willing to do whatever I had to. With Mama and the kids gone, it just didn't matter anymore. Besides, I'd have enough lonely days ahead to figure out those old nighttime promises.

The rain turned to drizzle before we got to town, then stopped altogether. Up ahead, I saw only a few people moving about, shaking out umbrellas, carrying on with their business.

Mr. Logan drove real slow around the square, and I leaned toward the window, staring up at the Van Zandt County Courthouse, the biggest building I'd ever seen. Three stories of red brick wrapped around a six-story central tower with a large copper eagle, wings spread, perched on the tallest peak.

We pulled up to the southwest corner of the square and parked by the Palace Drug Store. "There you go, miss. You'll find Doc Kellam's office inside. You need help with that bag?"

I shook my head. "I'm fine, Mr. Logan. Thank you for your kindness."

"My pleasure. Good luck to you." The young man tipped his stained felt hat and reached for his boxes.

I glanced around the square, half afraid I'd see wagons loaded with bodies, like the one Owen thought he'd seen, but the streets were clean and quiet, not nearly as busy as when I came to town with Papa on First Monday. I wondered if it was always this lifeless when trading days were over, or if people had just stayed away, fearful of catching the sickness.

I found the doctor's office inside the drug store and stepped through the door. A woman mopping floors looked up at me. "Doc won't be back till day after tomorrow," she said, "but you can leave a message."

"That long?" I asked.

"He left to check on the farms roundabout." She pointed to the desk behind her. "Can you write?"

I nodded.

"Then you'll find pen and paper there on the desk." She ducked her head and went back to her work.

I stepped around her mop bucket, disappointed, but I could at least tell the doctor about the Bonners and Dentons.

An old *Canton Herald* had been left open on the desktop, and as I reached for a pen, the word "influenza" caught my eye. "Spanish influenza," I read, "has now reached epidemic proportions in practically every state in the country."

Canton, too, according to the article. "Almost everyone is on the sick list," it said. "There hasn't been Sunday school or church either in some time on account of sickness. School is suspended for an indefinite time."

I skipped down the column.

"On Friday, November 29th, the death angel visited the home of Mr. and Mrs. Jack Dozier and claimed for his own, Lula Gafford. Oh, how we will miss her."

And farther down I read, "Saturday afternoon, November 30th, again the death angel visited our community at the home of Mr. Ed Boyd and claimed little Miss Edna Fudge. Edna was taken with influenza. To the bereaved we can only say, weep not for her for she was a sweet Christian girl and just before she died she said she was sleepy. Now she is asleep in Jesus where nothing can harm her."

The list went on and on. "M. H. Vandiver detained by daughter's severe illness. Mr. and Mrs. T. E. Campbell called home to their failing son—"

I looked away, refusing to read another painful account of that miserable sickness, and began my letter. "Dear Dr. Kellam," I wrote. "Mr. Bonner was very sick when I left him Saturday, and there has been at least one death in the Denton family. If you haven't already, would you please check on them as soon as you can?"

I signed the letter and gave the cleaning woman a nervous glance. I'd never had to look for work before and didn't have a single notion how to go about finding a position. "Um . . . excuse me, ma'am. I wonder if you could help me?"

She leaned on her mop and waited.

"I'm looking for work. Cooking, cleaning, caring for children—anything at all. Would you happen to know who might be hiring?"

She shook her head. "Ain't much to be had these days. Too many people dead and gone, and it's almost like they took the jobs with 'em."

I didn't quite understand what she meant by that, but I nodded anyway, thanked her, and headed off to the post office.

The muddy walks kept me watchful, but they couldn't keep me from dwelling on what I might do if there was no letter from Papa. By the time I stepped into the postmaster's line, dread billowed inside me, black as the clouds that hung over Canton. No matter how many foolish dreams I'd had of setting out on my own, I knew now that it was the last thing I wanted. Truth was, I'd been counting on Papa, banking on him to come for me. I remembered the morning he left, the clean scent of Mama's soap on him, the way he hugged me close like he didn't want to leave me, like he knew it could be the last time.

The last time.

I cringed, then blinked hard to stop the tears. There just *had* to be a letter in that post office. I needed my papa. He was all I had left.

A sign on the counter said the postmaster's name was Mr. McKinnon. "Can I help you?" he asked, peering at me over his small round spectacles.

"Yes, thank you. I'm looking for a letter addressed to the Kaplan family from my father, Jess Kaplan."

83

"I'll look," he said, and disappeared for a moment. He came back, shaking his head. "Sorry. There's nothing for you today."

"But, Mr. McKinnon, no one has picked up our mail in at least three weeks. Are you sure?"

"Sorry, miss. You can try again tomorrow if you like." He raised his eyes to the man standing in line behind me, and I moved out of the way.

The worry I'd been feeling turned to fear—knee-trembling, belly-quivering fear. With so much sickness sweeping across the country, Papa would've been worried about Mama and the kids, for sure. He would've been worried about me, too. Nothing would've kept him from writing or coming home. Nothing.

Unless he couldn't.

I TRIED TO SHAKE OFF the bad feelings, determined not to think about the possibility that Papa had gotten the sickness, too. After all, he'd always been so strong. I needed to remember that. If anyone could survive, it would be him. But the fear stayed, prowling around the edges of my hope like a hungry animal.

It was clear Papa couldn't help me now, and clear, too, that the money Miz Beulah gave me wouldn't last long. If I was going to make it on my own, I'd have to find work.

Even though the cleaning woman's words still haunted me, I decided to try the big hotel I'd seen down the street. The Dixie had three floors of rooms, and wide shady porches wrapped around both sides. When I came to town with Papa on First Monday, I'd heard someone say that Miss Mamie Maume had the "best lodgings and best food in these here parts." It must've been true. The Dixie was a fine-looking hotel, fine enough to make me jittery just pushing through the front door.

The smells coming from the kitchen filled the front hall, making my mouth water and my knees weak. I'd never paid for a meal in my life, but it wasn't hard to picture platters of fried chicken, mounds of mashed potatoes, and bowls of steaming gravy, all crowded together on a big table. Before I had a chance to imagine what the pies might be like, I spotted Miss Mamie, a round-faced, dark-haired woman with pretty eyes, sitting at a rolltop desk in the corner of the hall. She glanced up from her accounting books and gave me a sweeping look. I squirmed, remembering my mud-stained hem and lumpy flour sack.

"Can I help you, honey?" she asked simply.

It was a common courteous inquiry, but something in her friendly face said her words held more weight than they implied. The talk Mama'd had with me about heart signs jumped into my head, and I smiled. What if this fancy of Mama's worked on jobs, too? I'd felt something with Miss Mamie, just like I had with Miz Beulah, so maybe it wasn't such a far-fetched idea after all.

With renewed hope, I said, "Yes, thank you, ma'am. I'd like very much to apply for a position here if I may." I held out my reference. "I'd be willing to do most anything. As you can see, Mr. and Mrs. Bonner were very pleased with my work."

Miss Mamie read my letter and handed it back to me.

"Well, now, Miss Kaplan. That's probably one of the best letters I've ever seen. The Bonners sure do think highly of you. Problem is, my business is a bit sluggish now. It may take a while before the town is over the epidemic."

My hopes disappeared like smoke. I guess heart signs couldn't show a body how to find paying work.

I nodded my thanks, and she gave me a thoughtful look.

"Why don't you come on back in a few more weeks? Things just might look different by then."

"Thank you, Miss Mamie. I'll do that."

Disappointment must have colored my words, 'cause when I turned to go, she slipped her hand around mine and asked, "Are you hungry, honey?"

I was, but something made me shake my head. "I'm fine, Miss Mamie, but thank you all the same. I'll be looking forward to talking to you again real soon, though."

Miss Mamie nodded. "So will I, honey."

I stepped outside, closed the door behind me, and stood there, staring at the way the wood grain curled like smoke around the big brass handle. I already regretted not taking her up on her offer. Foolish pride wasn't going to feed my empty belly, that was for sure.

I understood now what the cleaning lady meant about the dead taking jobs with them. The epidemic must've hurt most every business in town. I mentally counted the coins tucked away in my pocket. Finding work might not be easy, if possible at all. I'd need to make my money last, and that meant finding a free place to sleep tonight if I wanted to keep eating.

I walked back to the Palace Drug Store and looked across the street to Hilliard's Mercantile. I'd try there next. Even if Mr. Hilliard didn't need anyone, he might know of someone who did.

A wagon rattled past, followed by an automobile, belching clouds of oily black smoke into the rain-washed air. I stepped off the curb, grabbed my skirt to guard it against splashes, and stopped cold.

This is no place to be hiking up your skirt like a tomboy, Mama scolded.

I stood there blinking like a fool while my heart did somersaults.

It was Mama's voice again. I'd heard her, just like this morning at the cabin, only this time it was no dream. I was wide awake. I looked behind me and both ways down the street. There was no one around, so where did the voice come from? Could a body just *will* something like this to happen?

I puzzled over it for a long moment, then finally shook my head. It really didn't matter. Having any small piece of my mama was a comfort right now, even if it was the part that fussed at me when I did something I shouldn't.

With Mama's words still swimming in my head, I smiled, dropped my skirt, and picked my way to the opposite walk to do what I had to do.

The Hilliard Mercantile had been in business since 1895, better than twenty years, according to the sign. I pushed through the door, jangling the tiny bell, and remembered my first time here. Surely the whole world was in this store. I smelled tangy pickles and smoked meats, tart apples and new fabrics. I saw chicken feed, rows of canned goods, and polished leather boots. And even though I couldn't see beyond the fishing poles, I was sure the coffins sat at the very back, just where they'd been the time before.

Mr. Hilliard was a man of impressive stature. I watched him raise a big hand and grab a twenty-five-pound bag of flour as easily as a box of crackers, then pull a tin of coffee off a high shelf behind him and place it in a box on the counter. "That brings the total to three dollars and thirty-seven cents, Cora," he said.

A woman dressed in black spilled coins from a velvet purse onto the counter and slowly counted them out with a gloved finger.

"I'll get Charlie to carry this out for you," Mr. Hilliard said, heading for the back of the store.

"Won't be necessary, George. Vera can bring it later."

He turned around and scooped up the coins. "I'll have it waiting for her, then. You take care of yourself and those children, Cora, and, again, my condolences. The town won't be the same without Sam."

The woman nodded and glided from the store, stirring hardly a jingle from the dangling bell.

With a grinding of gears, the register's drawer pinged and slid open. While the storekeeper sorted coins into the correct compartments, I plucked up my courage and stepped toward the counter.

"Hello, Mr. Hilliard." I pulled in a nervous breath. "My name is Mercy Kaplan."

His forehead wrinkled. "Mercy, you say?"

"Yessir."

"Oh sure, you must be the Bonners' hired girl. Monroe talks highly of you—you and them Denton boys who work for him."

The comment caught me off guard, but I liked knowing that Mr. Bonner had said nice things about me.

"Yessir," I said, smiling. "But they don't need me any longer, so I'm looking for new employment." I unfolded Miz Beulah's letter and placed it on the counter in front of him. "The Bonners were kind enough to write this reference for me."

Mr. Hilliard peered at the letter while butterflies danced inside me.

"It looks like a mighty fine letter, all right." He looked up at me and shrugged. "But with the influenza and all, I just don't have enough business to hire a clerk."

A lightheaded desperation pushed me closer to the counter. "But, Mr. Hilliard, I wouldn't mind doing just the sweeping and mopping if you could use me."

He shook his head. "Sorry, Mercy. Charlie takes care of that."

My hopes plunged. I nodded and thanked him, but before I reached the door he called after me. "Why don't you try down at the Glory?" he asked.

"The Glory?" My dancing butterflies returned.

"The Morning Glory Café, down the street. Go round back and see Emma Sayers. She'll probably be in the kitchen this time of day. Her business is slow, just like mine, but she lost help in the epidemic. Might be she could use you."

"Thank you, Mr. Hilliard." I gave him a grateful smile. "The Glory. I'll do that. Thank you very much."

The door seemed to give a happier jingle as I pushed

through and headed back down the street to the café. Maybe I'd have a dry place to sleep tonight after all.

I eased around puddles in the alley to the back of a white-washed brick building, found the steps to the kitchen door, and knocked.

A slender apron-clad woman with a chestnut braid circling the back of her head stepped up to the screen and pushed it open. "What can I do for you, honey?" she asked.

The woman wiped her heat-red cheeks with the back of her hand, leaving a streak of white flour across the side of her nose. I felt a sudden, nervous flurry. "Mrs. Sayers?" I asked.

"Just plain Emma will do, but you'd better hurry. I got cinnamon rolls in the oven."

"Yes'm." I struggled to center my thoughts on my purpose, reaching for the right words through my fear and the warm yeasty scent of fresh baked bread. "My name is Mercy Kaplan, and I'm looking for work. Mr. Hilliard sent me." I held out Miz Beulah's letter. "As you can see here, the Bonners thought highly of the job I did for them. I'm sure I can do as well for you if you'll take me on."

Breathless, I waited while the woman stared first at the paper trembling in my hand, then back at me, making me wonder if she could read the fear and hunger in my face. She raised a dusty white hand in a sudden motion for me to follow, and said, "Come on in."

When I stepped inside the screen door, she waved me to a chair beside a large worktable smeared with flour.

Eight loaves of fresh bread sat cooling on the cupboard, and when Emma checked the oven, I saw two big pans of cinnamon rolls browning inside. She reached for a folded cup towel, and while she pulled the rolls from the oven, I quickly cleared the flour from the table and spread out another towel.

Emma smiled and set the hot pans on the clean cloth.

"So the Bonners don't need you no more?" She fetched a bowl and began spreading creamy white frosting over the hot rolls. "Don't you have folks to help you out?"

I turned from the melting icing, awash in the sudden sharp memory of graves and pain. "No, ma'am," I told her. "My papa left months ago to find work, and . . . and my mama died from the influenza. Two sisters and a brother, too."

I'd said it fast, not wanting to leave time enough for the misery to well into tears again.

"I see," she said.

I waited, uncomfortable beneath Emma's sharp gaze. I had a feeling there was little that got past those eyes. I tried not to think about that—tried not to think of the warm rolls dripping with icing, either. I checked my posture, busied myself with straightening my skirt, then folded my hands in my lap.

"Well, Mercy, I'm sorry to say this place ain't doin' business enough to take on hired help right now." She scraped the last of the icing onto the rolls. "Since the epidemic, there's just me and my daughter, Beth, but we're managing."

I stared at her, wondering where I would go next, scared that, like for Papa, there would be nothing at all for me here in

Canton. I reached for my flour sack and stood to leave, barely remembering to thank her for her time.

"Now, wait," she said. "No need to get in a hurry. You could stay a spell so we could do some thinkin' on it. Could be we'll come up with an idea." Emma pulled a pitcher of milk from the icebox and smiled at me. "And while we're thinkin', we may as well try out these rolls 'fore they get cold."

Emma fed me, and then, to my surprise, she offered to let me stay awhile. In exchange for helping out, she said she'd give me meals and let me sleep in the storeroom off the kitchen.

"I know that's miserable pay, no two ways about it, but it's all I can do for you right now. And you should know that, even so, this ain't no job for slackers. With all the bad times of late, I was afraid we'd end up havin' to close the place, or, worse yet, get took by the influenza, too, like so many. But we're gettin' some of our business back now."

Relief swept through me like a sweet wind. I'd have a warm, dry place to sleep, at least for a while. "I'll do a good job for you, Emma, you'll see." I pushed up from the table and carried the glasses and empty pitcher to the sink to wash.

Emma busied herself with readying the dining room for the evening meal, and soon her daughter, Beth, came downstairs to help. The girl was pretty, with chestnut braids like her mama's, but there was something about her blue eyes that reminded me so much of Charity I found it hard to breathe around her. It didn't take long, though, to see that she was really nothing at all like Charity. She complained about having to work every day and gossiped about her friends each time Emma left the room. The second the door swung back open, she became the dutiful daughter again.

I smiled, and Emma gave us an appraising glance. "If people didn't know better, they'd think I had two daughters."

I looked again at Beth. Emma was right: We were enough alike to pass for family. All three of us.

Through the next four hours, I had little time for getting to know either of them any better. I peeled and chopped, cleared tables and washed dishes, and when there was no one else to feed, I cleaned up the spills from the stove and floors and took the trash out to the burning barrel.

Emma and Beth went upstairs with a tray when the work was finished, but I was too tired to eat the meal I'd earned. I spread the blankets Emma gave me on the floor of the store-room and turned out the light, grateful for the ache in my shoulders and the drowsiness that already weighed heavy on my eyelids. I just wanted to go to sleep, fast and deep, before my thoughts could turn toward home.

chapter
15

"I DON'T CARE. I'm not going back to that place!"

The voice coming from the dining room sounded a bit like Beth's, but I knew it couldn't be her. The girl had just gone out back to the burning barrel.

"It's okay, honey. Your papa will understand."

"No, he won't, Emma. He'll make me go back, I know he will!"

The girl sobbed, and I caught myself straining to catch Emma's words, crooned too low to be heard from the kitchen. It was then I heard Mama again.

Shame on you, Mercy Kaplan. Papa and I taught you better.

With surprise, I felt my cheeks flush hot. That scolding was exactly what I would've heard if Mama had really caught me eavesdropping. I jumped away from the door and busied myself with slicing bacon for the morning meal.

Beth pushed open the back door and paused, ears trained toward the excitement in the dining room. "What's happening?" she asked.

I chose not to answer, offering only a shrug instead, determined not to bring on another rebuke from Mama for gossiping.

Beth would have to find out on her own, but she didn't seem to have a problem with that. She tiptoed across the floor to listen, then quickly disappeared through the door.

The hushed voices picked up, but after a few moments, Emma returned to the kitchen. I watched her from the corner of my eye, curious about the vigorous way she dumped flour into her large copper bowl, then added salt, leavening, and lard. She was only mixing the morning biscuits, but there was something in the *click, click, click* of her gold band against the rounded bowl that made me decide right then to stay out of her way.

Breakfast business went smoothly, and Emma and her daughter appeared to shrug off the strange early-morning difficulty. They even lingered briefly with me after the noon rush, talking. They wanted to know more about me.

"There's not much to tell," I said. "I hope to hear something from my father soon, and I want to check with Doc Kellam when he gets back to town to see if he looked in on the Bonners and Dentons." I glanced up at them and forced a smile, hesitant to say more. I didn't want to tell them about the note I'd found on the mantel, about the four graves under the oak. I didn't want to cry. Instead, I asked Emma about how she came to own the Glory.

She shrugged. "Beth's father died 'fore she was born, but he left enough to pay down on the café."

Like me, Emma seemed reluctant to say more, so I didn't pry. She appeared to be a woman of few words, a quality her daughter hadn't inherited. Once Beth opened her mouth, she was like a dog with a bone, worrying a bit of gossip to death till there wasn't a scrap left to chew on.

Yet I found myself wishing I knew more about Emma. I couldn't help but wonder why she chose to wear a wedding band if her husband had passed on all those years ago.

The wind turned cold that evening, gusting around windows and doors like it envied the cozy warmth we'd found. Slowly it gave up and inched away, leaving a crisp, still night, reminding me of Christmas and the snowflake garlands Charity loved to cut from white paper. I'd never been able to accomplish the delicate cuts like she had, though she'd tried to teach me often enough.

It was already December 10. I looked around the kitchen, wondering where I'd be when Christmas arrived this year. It really didn't matter much where I ended up, though. That day would never again be the same for me.

On this chilly evening, Emma kept a stew simmering at the back of the stove, along with a pot of chicken and dumplings, and before the night was over, she'd served up most all of it.

When the kitchen and dining room were finally clean, I crawled onto my pallet in the storeroom, achy tired again, but thinking about tomorrow. Emma had said I should leave in the afternoon, before the supper work began, and try to catch Doc Kellam in his office. I planned to check with the post office again, too.

I pulled my quilt to my chin, eager for sleep to take me, but a pounding jerked me to my feet. My thoughts leapfrogged to the night Owen died. I glanced up the stairs, full of dread. Had Emma heard it?

I shrugged off my nightgown, hurried to dress again, then peered into the dining room. Light from a streetlamp had turned the white table linens to yellow shrouds, and through the oval glass in the front door, I saw a shadow.

The pounding sounded again, urgent enough to bring Emma scurrying down the stairs in her bare feet and robe. Beth followed close behind, her unbraided hair kinky and swishing around her back.

"I'm coming, I'm coming," Emma called, hurrying on her toes across the cold floor. She unbolted the door, and a young girl with red braids fell into her arms.

"Emma," she bawled, "I don't know what to do!"

It was the voice I'd heard before daybreak this morning. I slipped back to the kitchen, determined not to repeat my earlier blunder, but this time Emma followed, dragging the freckle-faced girl behind her.

"Mercy, warm up that tea on the back of the stove, and, Vera, you sit down here and talk so's I can make some sense of all this."

Beth slid into a seat at the far end of the table and pulled herself up small and quiet, reminding me of the times I'd done the same at home when I didn't want to be sent from the room. Sometimes Mama and Papa would forget I was there.

Emma sat herself down knee to knee with Vera, and said, "What happened this time?"

"It's Mrs. Wilder again, Emma. I just can't work for that woman anymore. Little Gabe turned up missing tonight, and she said I was to blame."

Vera broke into sobs again, prompting Emma to pull a handkerchief from the sleeve of her robe and shove it into the girl's hand. "Please stop blubberin', Vera, and start from the beginnin', or we ain't never gonna figure all this out."

The girl nodded, blew her nose, then took a sip of the tea I placed in front of her. "The night started out just fine," she said, still sniffling. "I made sure the children got their baths, and afterward I read them their Bible story. Gilly acted silly and couldn't sit still—after all, she's only four—but Gabe was such a sweetheart. He listened like he understood every word. He's really bright for a five-year-old, don't you think?"

Emma twitched with annoyance. "Just get on with it, Vera."

"Well, when I was through, I left their door open a crack so I could hear if there was a problem, then I went into Mrs. Wilder's room to turn down her bed. After that, I checked again on the children. They were quiet, so I didn't see no reason to worry. I went on downstairs then to finish up in the kitchen. I washed the dishes, mopped the floor, and sorted laundry for wash day tomorrow." Vera's chin quivered. "When I went back upstairs, he . . . he was gone."

The girl erupted into sobs again, and Emma's eyes rolled. "Keep going, Vera. Then what?"

Vera wiped away her tears and drew a deep breath. "That's when Mrs. Wilder started yelling at me. Daniel came hobbling out on his crutches, trying to quiet her enough so he could find out what was going on, but she just wouldn't stop. She kept hollering about how I shoulda been more watchful. But,

Emma, when Daniel finally understood what happened, that boy never said a single mean word to me. He just started looking all over the house for his little brother."

"Yes, yes, we all know how thoughtful Daniel can be. So where did you find the boy?"

"We didn't. That's why Mrs. Wilder sent me for help."

"Well, for gosh sakes, Vera! Why didn't you say that in the first place?" Emma pushed up from the table, eyes darting like a hunting hound's, already deciding on who should do what. "Beth, you run tell George Hilliard to gather up some folks while I get my clothes on. Vera, you help Mercy get together some coffee and those doughnuts I made today. It could be a long night."

Emma headed up the stairs, but paused and turned, toes crimped over the edge of the step. "Mercy, get your coat on, girl. You can go with us."

She fussed the whole time we were making coffee and packing up doughnuts, saying Mr. Hilliard and half the town would likely be there ahead of us, but we finally got out the door, all of us with our arms full.

Outside, the raw north wind had blown away clouds, leaving the sky clear and starry and the muddy road skimmed with ice. I followed Emma and Vera through the yellow circles cast by the town's streetlights and into the dark, all the while wondering what could've made such a small boy leave his warm bed.

BY THE TIME we got to the Wilders', people had already gathered around the wide front porch, just as Emma had suspected. Mr. Hilliard was busy dividing them into search parties and sending them out in different directions. Voices rose and fell, calling out for Gabe, and lanterns flashed in the distance like wild cat eyes.

Emma set her big basket of doughnuts on the porch and waited till the last of the volunteers had been sent out before she asked where Daniel was.

"Out looking, I guess." Mr. Hilliard shoved a lantern into Emma's hand. "Cora's inside, though."

"Yeah. Figured she would be." Emma blew out a frustrated breath, and I had to wonder why that bit of news had irritated her so.

"What section do you want us to take, George?" she asked.

"Check the areas around the carriage house and the chicken pens. If you come across Daniel, try to get him back to the house. He sure don't need to be out in the dark with that bad leg of his."

Emma nodded and motioned for me and Vera to follow her

out back. We checked every inch of the carriage house, then moved on to the chicken pens. Emma didn't hesitate to brush away roosting hens, setting off a flurry of wings and squawks so loud we almost missed the call for help. When the chickens settled, I heard it.

"Over here!" a voice called.

Emma scrambled from the pen and shouted back, "That you, Daniel? You got Gabriel with you?"

"Yeah! By the garden shed. Hurry!"

She held her lantern high to light the way and called over her shoulder: "Get up to the house, Vera, and let George know we may need help. Mercy, you come with me."

Emma wasn't a large woman, but she plowed through the overgrown garden like a workhorse while I struggled to keep up. My shoes broke through the thin icy covering and sank, squishing into the muddy soil. Up ahead I spotted a dim halo of light coming from behind a small building.

"Is he okay, Daniel?" Emma called.

I listened, but there was no answer. Just before we reached the shed, light from Emma's lantern flashed across a broken crutch stuck in the mud, and farther on, we came across another, discarded in the frosty brown grass. We rounded the corner of the building, and I saw a boy who couldn't be much older than me, shivering on the cold ground, his coat wrapped around his younger brother.

"Gabe won't wake up," Daniel said.

His words sounded thick with cold and fear, and I could

almost feel them break inside me like the ice crunching beneath my shoes.

Emma swung the lantern toward me, and I caught the worried look in her eyes.

"Unbutton your coat, Mercy."

She set the lantern on the ground, lifted the boy from his brother's arms, and handed him to me. "Hold him close, now, and get him up to the house while I help Daniel."

I hugged the small, cold boy to my body, and for a moment I couldn't move. He reminded me too much of Justice.

"Don't dally," she cautioned. "He needs warmin' up."

I wrapped my coat tightly around him and headed back across the garden, but I didn't have far to go. Vera had alerted Mr. Hilliard, and I could already see his lantern rushing toward me.

When he reached me he took the boy, and I was surprised at the emptiness he left behind.

"Tell Daniel I reached Doc Kellam; he's on his way. And I already sent word to the searchers that they can go on home, too."

I nodded, annoyed at the tears welling up in my eyes. I swiped at them with my coat sleeve, and with a last glance at Gabe, I turned toward the shed. As I neared Emma's light, I shouted out Mr. Hilliard's message.

"Good," Emma grunted. "You can go, too. We'll be along soon."

I turned to leave, but not before seeing the lantern lurch and go out. I took off across the dark garden, guided by a flurry of words I couldn't quite make out. When I got there, Emma was helping Daniel off the ground, a faceless shadow struggling to regain footing in the slippery mud.

"Oh, quit your bellyachin', Daniel. You know there ain't no other way."

She steadied him while he balanced his weight on his one good leg, but even in the dark, I could tell she needed help. I sidled up to them, slipped a hand around the boy's cold back, and flinched at the sudden closeness. He didn't seem to notice, though. He stretched an arm across my shoulder and brought his face even closer. His bristly chin brushed my forehead, and his breath puffed into the frosty night, smelling faintly of sweet peppermint.

Emma and I strained, slowly making progress. Each time Daniel's weight shifted, I felt his body tense and move beneath my hands, hard and muscled, like old Tucker when he pulled a plow. Something about the boy's nearness drew me even closer, and for a moment, I leaned in to him, comfortable in the curve of his arm and the way my cheek rested against his shoulder. As if I belonged there.

Stunned at where my thoughts had led me, I pulled back hard, almost making him fall.

"Sorry," I whispered, fearing he might feel the heat of my embarrassment right through his clothing.

He grunted.

I concentrated on the rhythm of our five-legged gait, and together we worked our way across the garden toward the chicken pens.

By the time we reached the house, Doc Kellam had arrived. I wished I could ask him about the Bonners and Dentons, but with everyone so worried, I knew this wasn't the right time. Tomorrow would have to do.

I stepped aside so the men could help Daniel up the steps and into the parlor, but just before letting me go, he gave me a green-eyed glance and nodded his thanks, setting off a heart-stopping flurry inside me. This wasn't the usual butterflies. It felt more like a stampede of wild horses.

I steadied myself against the porch railing, trying to figure out what had just happened, and then it hit me. I'd been betrayed. Betrayed by my wandering thoughts. And by my own body, for heaven's sake! I blew out a furious breath and willed the foolish churning away. After all, other than a love for his little brother and those emerald eyes, there seemed to be nothing in Daniel that set him above any of the boys I'd met or heard about. I needed to remember that.

I waited by the steps, but I couldn't help watching what was happening inside. The men wrapped Daniel in a blanket and settled him into a chair next to the settee where his brother lay cocooned in quilts. I looked for the four-year-old sister Vera spoke of, but I saw no other children in the room.

Emma leaned in close. "You go on back to the Glory, Mercy, and get some sleep. I'll stay and see what Doc Kellam has to say about Gabriel."

I glanced at Vera. She was red-eyed and teary, and Emma must've seen my concern.

"Don't worry," she said. "I'll take care of Vera."

I didn't want to leave, but I nodded anyway and took one last look at the people gathered in the parlor. Daniel pushed a lock of dark, curly hair from his brother's forehead, just like I'd seen Mama do for Justice so many times, and a sharp longing for my only brother stabbed right through me.

I pulled away from the window and the pain, but not before noticing a woman in black standing at the back of the room, the same woman I'd seen in Mr. Hilliard's store yesterday, the one who'd recently lost her husband in the epidemic. Cora, he'd called her. Emma had mentioned her by name, too, just hours ago, when we arrived. She had to be the mother.

She looked delicate and quite pretty, standing beside a small writing desk in the far corner of the room, but there was something odd in the way she seemed obsessed with a cluster of yellow pencils sitting in a blue china cup.

Emma opened the front door a crack and called out to her, but the woman never stirred. She just stood there, moving the pencils first this way, then that, lost in her own thoughts.

"To gain that which is worth having,
it may be necessary to lose everything."

BERNADETTE DEVLIN

chapter
17

A LOT OF head shaking and fervent speculation about little Gabe's mishap floated freely among the Glory patrons the next morning, but no one seemed to know how or why he ended up in the cold behind the shed. Or if they did, they didn't say.

Emma had come home late last night and gone straight to bed. I'm sure she didn't know I was lying awake in the dark storeroom, wondering about Gabe, or she would've stopped to let me know what Doc Kellam had to say. All my worry and guesswork turned out to be a blessing of sorts, however. It kept my mind off my own troubles. It wasn't till we were in the kitchen the next morning, working on breakfast, that she told me the boy was okay. I also found out that Cora was indeed the mother, and that Daniel was nineteen.

"Daniel has worked in his daddy's repair shop every day after school since he was little," Beth said. "With Mr. Wilder's passing, though, he took to running the business himself."

She sat down at the table to peel potatoes, and when Emma disappeared into the dining room, Beth told me more.

"Poor Daniel has had his hands full, working and trying to

keep up with those two little ones," she whispered. "And Lord knows they've needed him, with their mama the way she is."

"What do you mean?"

"Why, everyone in town knows Miz Cora ain't right in the head. Might be 'cause her mama died such a horrible death, getting trampled by horses and all, but whatever the reason, she does strange things, that woman. Vera said she's seen Miz Cora put something on to cook and then just walk away to play games with the kids like she was ten all over again, leaving supper to burn. Poor Vera has to follow her around, checking on everything she does."

I frowned, remembering the pencils in the blue china cup.

"Vera thinks she had something to do with Daniel's broken leg, too, 'cause he won't say a word about how it happened." She looked up at me. "He's not her own, you know. His mama died when he was little, and then his daddy married Miz Cora about six years ago." She picked up another potato. "It's a puzzle why that man wanted to marry someone like her, 'less'n it was for the bit of money her mama left her." She shook her head. "The woman is just too strange. No wonder poor Mr. Wilder passed on in the epidemic. He probably saw it as a welcome relief."

"Beth!"

Emma stood in the dining-room doorway, red-faced, eyes glinting with fury. She stormed to the worktable and grabbed her daughter by the arm. "I'll *not* have you spreadin' nasty gossip," she hissed. "That poor family's burdens are great enough without you heapin' on another!"

Beth cringed. "I'm sorry, Mama. It won't happen again; I promise."

Emma stared at her long and hard before releasing her arm. "You just better see that it don't," she said.

I ducked my head and turned back to the pancake batter I'd started.

ALONG ABOUT TWO in the afternoon, Emma came to tell me that the sheriff had seen Doc Kellam in his office just ten minutes before.

"Get that apron off, Mercy, and go," she said.

I flung my apron on the worktable, ran to the Palace Drug Store, and burst through the doctor's door. "Dr. Kellam," I called.

I looked for the cleaning woman I'd seen before, but the office appeared to be empty. "Dr. Kellam," I called again. "Are you in?"

A man stepped from the back, holding a shiny violin in one hand and a polishing cloth in the other. "I'm here," he said. "What can I do for you?"

"I'm sorry to disturb you, Dr. Kellam, but I'm Mercy Kaplan. I left you a note the other day."

He nodded, set his violin aside, and gave me a curious glance. "Didn't I see you at the Wilders' last night?"

"Yessir. I've been helping Emma at the café. But about my letter . . . I'm very worried about Mr. Bonner. The Dentons, too. Did you happen to look in on them?"

He gave me a penetrating look. "Are you family?"

I shook my head. "I was the Bonners' hired girl. Owen and Garrett Denton worked for them, too, but I was sent away when Mr. Bonner got sick."

He nodded. "Well, you're a very lucky girl. Half the Denton family has passed from the influenza, and we went back to bury Monroe and Beulah just this morning."

His words knocked the wind out of me. Unspeakable visions of the Bonners dying alone shuddered through me. I dropped into a chair and covered my face with my hands.

"Here, here, now," Dr. Kellam crooned. "I thought you said you were just the hired girl."

I swallowed hard and tried to speak around the knot in my throat. "They were all I had left," I whispered.

His eyes softened, and he gave me a knowing nod. "Lots of folks around here are in the same boat, Mercy, but Emma's a good woman. She'll see you through it."

My head bobbed in agreement, but I knew Emma couldn't help me. No one could. First Mama and the kids, and now the Bonners—all of them just gone. The loss stabbed deep, and I felt my frail hope for Papa bleeding away.

Papa.

I blinked back the tears and raised my head. "I . . . I have to go," I mumbled. "Thank you, Dr. Kellam. For the news and for your kind concern."

I headed for the door, regret tumbling wild inside me at the way I'd left the Bonners that dark morning. But right now, I had to get to the post office. I had to know if Papa was safe.

Once there, I stood in line at the counter, fear thumping so fierce in my chest I could hardly speak Papa's name when it was my turn.

Mr. McKinnon checked the incoming mail and shook his head. "Sorry, miss. Maybe tomorrow."

I stared at him a moment, then stumbled back out to the street, knowing full well there'd be no letter for me tomorrow. Or the next day. Or even next week. I'd been a fool, making excuses, hiding from the awful truth. Papa never wrote a letter because he couldn't. He was gone, just like Mama and the kids, just like the Bonners and Dentons.

I'd lost everyone.

That shattering finality stabbed through me, over and over again, till I was sure my heart would never stop bleeding.

I DIDN'T WANT to go back to the questions waiting for me at the Glory, but I had no place else to go. I felt numb, lost in my own darkness, thoughts flitting like goose down in a fickle breeze.

Expecting the worst, I stepped through the back door, picked up a paring knife, and reached for a potato like a drowning person grasping at a drifting log. Emma took one look and let me be. I guess she knew I needed the reassuring rhythm of familiar work.

It wasn't till everything was done and Beth had gone upstairs with her tray that Emma sat me down and said simply, "What can I do?"

I shook my head, and though I'd been determined not to allow even one more tear, the pure pain of it all rolled down my cheeks anyway. Emma waited till I found my voice, then listened while I tried to explain how I'd come to care so much for the Bonners.

"But there's more." I looked up at her. "There's been no word from Papa, and now I have no choice but to believe the worst. With so much sickness around, he would've written if he could've. He's gone, Emma." I buried my face in my hands. "They're *all* gone."

She hugged me while I cried again, and for a moment, it was Mama's arms I felt around me; it was Mama's warm breath on my cheek. "I don't want to be alone," I whispered to her, but it wasn't Mama who heard my words. It was Emma.

She pulled back to look at me. "You ain't never gonna be alone, Mercy Kaplan, unless you choose to be." She hugged me again, then brought a bowl of chicken and dumplings to the table. "You eat a little something before you turn in, you hear? And if you need *anything* tonight, even just a little company, you come on up to my room, okay?"

I managed a nod and a small spoonful of soup to please her, but when she was gone, I pushed the bowl back. I couldn't eat another bite.

Later, under my quilt, I thought about what she'd said, but I knew she was wrong. I hadn't chosen to be alone. The sickness had done that for me, all by itself, fulfilling my long-ago wish.

I was on my own.

chapter
18

THE NIGHT HAD brought no peace, yet, the next morning, I found myself folding my pallet, dressing, and starting breakfast as if nothing had changed. I soon realized, however, that the numbness that had gotten me through the night had also dulled my sight and slowed my movements, till even I had to accept that I wouldn't be much help today. Still, Emma didn't complain.

Somehow I managed to get through the next days. Then, on Sunday, Vera marched right into the kitchen, and everything changed.

"I quit," she said, her face a strange combination of fear and satisfaction. "I just couldn't take Mrs. Wilder another minute, Emma, but I haven't told Papa yet. What do you think he'll do?"

Emma shrugged. "What do *you* think he'll do? Beat you?"

Vera frowned and shook her head. "You know Papa doesn't do that sort of thing, but he'll be mad, I'm sure."

"Of course he will, but he'll get over it." Emma's eyes narrowed. "Vera, why don't you take Mercy's apron and finish frying up that bacon for me before you go home."

Vera and I both gave Emma a puzzled look.

"I've got an errand, and Mercy is the one who needs to do it."

With a nod, Vera tied on my apron, and I followed Emma upstairs to her bedroom. She pulled a dress from her closet and draped it across the bed.

"The washbasin is right there. Help yourself to my brush and combs, and when you're all cleaned up, put on that dress, and get out to the Wilders'. Tell Cora I sent you to replace Vera."

"But—"

"No buts, Mercy. You need a paying position, and that's something I can't give you right now. Later, when business gets better, you can come back if you want, but for now you'd better go see about that job."

Emma was right. I started to thank her, but she'd already headed back downstairs.

I stood there, looking at her room. There wasn't a speck of dust anywhere, but, like with Emma herself, something was always out of place. I picked up scissors and thread, put them back in the tumbled sewing basket, then tucked her mended stockings into a dresser drawer. When I turned, I caught my full image in a tall cheval mirror that stood in the corner. It was a curious experience, like looking at a stranger. I couldn't remember ever seeing myself all in one piece like that, except maybe in a wavy store-window. Easing closer, I played with my image, moving my chin, my arms, and finally turning on my toes to look over my shoulder.

I'd never thought of myself as pretty. I was tall and thin, and my hair was plain brown, far from the honey gold that inspired poets and admirers. I cocked my head to one side and saw Papa's firm chin. And Mama's blue eyes, set large and wide, peered back at me from my own pale-moon face. I had Mama's nose, too, even if it did have a light dusting of freckles, but I'd never be as pretty as she was.

I unbraided my hair and brushed it till it fell smooth and silky, then pulled it up and fastened it into a knot with Emma's ivory combs, the way Mama always wore hers. I washed my face and neck in the white china basin, then slipped into the dark blue dress she'd left for me, smoothing the white crocheted collar and cuffs till they were perfect. It was a beautiful dress, far nicer than anything I'd ever owned. I checked my reflection, but this time I saw something I'd never seen before.

"Oh, Mama," I whispered, fixing my eyes on the fully dressed image in the mirror, "I look like you."

My throat tightened, prompting me to turn away before the tears could start. I had no time for sentimental foolishness. I slipped on my coat and hurried out to the road.

The weather had turned warmer, and the sunshine seemed to have a positive effect on the few townspeople that were about. Men tipped their hats, ladies smiled and nodded, and I even heard a laugh rise above the occasional clatter of street noise.

At the edge of town I saw a sign on a whitewashed brick building that said *Wilder's Repair*, only it wasn't the simple fix-it shop I'd imagined. Before the epidemic, Mr. Wilder had repaired automobiles and wagons. Two high windows watched the road like big eyes, and the open wooden doors sagged between them in a jack-o'-lantern frown. Though the sign said they were closed on Sundays, someone was obviously there. I peeked inside. The large, open garage felt as cool as a cave and smelled of grease and gasoline, but mostly it was just quiet. I paused, curious, and when I didn't see anyone about, I took a tentative step over the threshold.

I peered past a blocked-up Model T on the far left, to the shelves and cluttered worktables at the back, and then noticed a wagon with a missing wheel sitting by a blacksmith forge. A sudden clatter from under the automobile made me jump, and I backed away quick. I wasn't at all ready to explain why I was here, especially when I didn't even know myself. I hurried back out to the road and went on my way.

I hadn't noticed the Wilders' house much the night we searched for Gabe, only that it was set far off the road at the edge of town. I soon glimpsed its clapboard siding shining white under a bright winter sun. The house was a pretty two-story with wraparound porches that dripped wooden lace, just the kind Mama had loved, and suddenly, more than ever, I wanted this job. My heart quickened, and my hands grew clammy.

Some people sense fear, Mercy. You'd best keep your wits about you.

It was Mama again. Or maybe it was me, remembering Mama. I couldn't tell. I pulled in a deep breath to calm my nerves, deciding to do justice to the good advice, no matter where it came from.

While crossing the tidy porch, I caught sight of a blue china cup discarded near the front door. I stared at it, uneasy. It was full of yellow pencils, all of them snapped in two. With difficulty, I pulled my gaze from the splintered pieces, raised a hesitant hand to the door, and knocked.

The curtain at the side window moved, and a small face peered out at me, but only for a moment. It appeared to be the four-year-old girl that Vera had called Gilly. A muffled voice sent the child to another room to play, and when the door finally opened, I found myself face to face with Mrs. Cora Wilder.

"Yes?" she asked.

"Good morning, Mrs. Wilder," I said more bravely than I felt. "My name is Mercy Kaplan. Emma Sayers told me that you might need someone soon to help out with the children and the house. I'd be very pleased if you'd consider me for that position."

She gave me a vacant stare, reminding me of the creek after a long, hard rain. You could never tell where the perilous holes were under all that muddy water. She blinked, stepped back, and swung the door wide. "Please, come in."

I smiled my thanks, followed her into the parlor, and seated myself on a heavily brocaded love seat. While I watched her settle onto the edge of a wingback chair, I had to wonder if all those peculiar stories Beth told me were true. This woman appeared to be quite composed and sure of herself. She certainly didn't seem to be absentminded enough to leave supper burning while she ran off to play with the children.

"Emma sent you?" she asked.

"Yes, ma'am. She thinks I could handle your needs quite well."

Mrs. Wilder nodded, and I saw a slight smile lift the corners of her mouth. "Emma would certainly know that better than anyone." She rose from her chair. "When can you start?"

The question startled me. I hadn't expected to be hired so quickly, and without even a confirmation from Emma. "I . . . I suppose I should at least finish out the day at the Glory. Would tomorrow morning be soon enough?"

She nodded. "Anytime tomorrow would be fine. The pay is four dollars and fifty cents a week with room and board, and you'll have every Wednesday off."

"Yes, ma'am. And my duties?"

"You'll tend to the children's needs, of course, and do a share of the cooking and housework. Daniel and I will help out occasionally, so that you won't be overly burdened. After all, the children's play is important, too, and they'll look forward to having you join them."

"Yes, ma'am." I smiled, already feeling better about this woman. I followed her to the door, thinking that Beth had to be wrong. Vera, too. Mrs. Wilder did appear cool and aloof, surely not an uncommon stance when dealing with hired help, but I didn't see a single thing strange about her.

I stepped onto the porch, and when I turned to thank her, the toe of my shoe hit the blue china cup, knocking it over. Broken bits of yellow rolled everywhere.

"Oh, no," she whispered. "Look what I've done." She scrambled to pick up the splintered pieces.

"Please, Mrs. Wilder; it was my fault. Let me get them." I gathered up the last of the spilled pencils and held out the cup. "There," I said. "All is right again."

She backed away, her face a mask. I wasn't sure what to do.

"Um . . . maybe I'll just set them here by the door for you," I told her, "right where they were." I bent to set the cup down and rose in time to see the door click shut in my face.

ALL THE WAY BACK to the Glory, I wondered if I should tell Emma about Mrs. Wilder's odd behavior, but before I finally stepped through the door, I'd decided to let it be. I had a real paying job now, my first ever. It was what I wanted, what I needed, and I planned to do my best for that family. Mama would expect no less from me, and if things didn't work out, I could come back to the Glory. Emma had assured me of that.

Beth gave me a surprised look when I announced my news, but Emma seemed pleased.

She sat down at the worktable, saying, "Cora's the lucky one. Those kids, too. You'll be a blessing to 'em, no doubt. When do you start?"

"Tomorrow."

I didn't want to be a burden to Emma any longer than I had

to, but just being back in her kitchen had drained away a portion of my eagerness. I hadn't realized till that moment how much she'd come to mean to me in so little time. Leaving wouldn't be easy.

"Monday's a good day for startin' a new job," she said.

"I'll be off every Wednesday. I'd be happy to come back and help out."

She laughed. "Believe me, you'll need the rest by then. Cora ain't the easiest woman to work for, as I'm sure you know by now."

"Do you know her well?" I asked.

She gave me a hesitant look, as if weighing just how much she wanted to confide.

"I was younger than you when I went to work for her parents," she said finally, "so I guess you could say I knew them well enough. We all grew up in Martin's Mill, not far from here."

"All?"

"Me, Cora, and her brother, Devon."

I nodded. "Does her brother still live there?"

Emma blinked a few times, then gave me a blank stare. "Devon's dead. Been gone a long time now."

I wanted to hear more, but something in Emma's eyes made me wary of prying further. In an abrupt move, she pushed back her chair and strode into the dining room.

The rest of the day remained busy enough to keep my mind

centered on kitchen work—a relief, with thoughts of death and loss always so close. Still, the worry over my new position haunted me, too. Mr. Bonner had been a challenge, but at least I knew where I stood during those first weeks, and in the end, he'd treated me like family. Mrs. Wilder promised to be far more difficult. I wasn't at all sure I could keep her happy. According to Vera, the woman blew this way and that, calm one moment, then blustery the next. How could a body ever stay ahead of something like that?

Late that night, after Emma and Beth had turned in, I felt a sick restlessness, caught between my anxiety about tomorrow and a longing for something—anything—familiar. I reached for the flour sack sitting at the foot of my pallet, then slid my hand inside, across Justice's tin soldier and down to the corner of Charity's diary. I wanted to read her words again, hear her voice in my head, but I was afraid of where the pages might take me, afraid I'd sink so deep into grief's black mire I might never get out.

Oh, but I missed her so.

I ran a finger around the edge of the cover, and with a surge of courage, I pulled out the notebook.

"*The Private Diary of Charity Theophilia Kaplan,*" I read.

I had to smile. She'd always hated her middle name, and though she could've easily left it out, there it was.

"It means God's beloved," Mama would tell her every time she complained. "Your papa chose it just for you."

But nothing could soothe her irritation. "You shoulda stopped him, Mama," she always replied. "Now I'm stuck with it forever."

"Forever," I whispered, and turned to the first entry.

August 7, 1917
She's here! Mama and Papa named her Honor Juliana Kaplan. She is so beautiful and tiny, like a china doll, and Mercy helped the midwife with the birth. I'd be overcome with fear for sure, but I bet Mercy never even flinched. I wish I could be more like my sister. She is always so brave, and I don't think there's anything she can't do.

The sobs rushed in from nowhere, swallowing me up, sucking my breath away, and my heart rebelled in great thumps.

It's not true, I wanted to scream at her. This I *can't* do, not without you. And I'm *not* brave, Charity.

I pushed my wet face into my pillow.

I'm not brave at all.

chapter 19

I CHASED SLEEP all night, longing for forgetfulness, and though it seemed I'd never once closed my eyes, I must've slept, for I dreamed of Charity. We sat together in the tall, green grass under the shady oak at home while she read to me. It was a sweet dream, for there were no graves, and when I woke, I could finally turn my thoughts to what lay ahead.

I rose well before Emma and Beth, eager to put this dark night behind me, but I was already dreading not seeing Emma every day. In the short time I'd spent here, I'd come to depend on her, not just for a roof over my head and food in my belly, but for the warmth in her eyes and the reassurance in her smile. I didn't feel quite so alone when she was near.

I braided my hair and wrapped it around my head like Emma wore hers, then I dressed, packed my flour sack, and folded the blankets I'd used as a pallet. Careful not to wake anyone, I started on breakfast. By the time Emma came downstairs, ready to work, I had potatoes peeled, cut, and waiting in cool water; bacon, sausage, and ham ready for the skillet; and a big bowl of pancake batter covered with a cup towel.

Emma shook her head and mumbled, "That Cora better treat you right, or I'll be comin' to fetch you back."

Smiling, I pulled out the big mixing bowl Emma used for biscuits, but she plucked it from my hands.

"I'll do that," she said. "You've done enough already. You need to get going." She held Miz Beulah's coat while I slipped it on, then blew out a long breath. "You sure don't make good-byes easy, do you?" She pulled me close in a warm hug.

"I just wish I knew how to thank you," I whispered.

"Hush, now," she said, pulling back to point a finger at me. "You just remember to tell Cora that I want you here on Christmas Day, you hear?"

I nodded, grateful, and Emma followed me through the dining room and out the door. With a wave, I left her standing in the doorway, watching me leave, just like Mama had done the last time I saw her.

I HAD EXPECTED THAT, with so many losses from the sickness, few people would feel like celebrating Christmas, but store windows all over town sparkled with tinsel this Monday morning. For some, Christmas would still come, but for me, the magic surrounding that day had vanished with Papa. Gone. Buried with Mama and the kids.

I had no interest in garlands or carols or gifts, but I was thankful for this early walk, for the bit of time to clear my head and point my thoughts in a new direction. With all the sudden changes I'd had to face, I couldn't help wondering what would be waiting for me this time.

I neared Wilder's Repair, and though I had no intention of repeating my earlier close call, I couldn't help but slow my step and peer inside again. This time I saw crutches leaning against the Model T, and when I looked closer, I saw a wave of dark hair under the running board.

It had to be Daniel. I hurried on before he had a chance to see me, yet even that brief glimpse troubled me. The thought of living in the same house with him made me uneasy, maybe even more so than trying to please Mrs. Wilder. At least he'd be off working most every day. His stepmother, on the other hand, would be right there, watching everything I did. I remembered how Mrs. Wilder thought it was Vera's fault that Gabe had turned up missing, and my stomach gave a nervous flutter. I didn't know what I'd do in a situation like that.

No sense fretting over things that haven't happened.

It was Mama's voice in my head again. I'd heard her say that very thing to me more times than I could remember, and I suppose she was right. Things rarely turned out as dreadful as I imagined.

By the time I reached the house, I was feeling somewhat better. I never liked doing chores at home, but I was a good worker, probably better than Vera. I'd win Mrs. Wilder over. I'd find a way to win them all over.

I stepped onto the porch and noticed that the china cup of

broken pencils was gone. I took that as a good sign and rapped on the door.

Mrs. Wilder greeted me with a smile and a generous dusting of flour on her apron.

"Come in! We're all in the kitchen." She waved for me to follow. "We've been baking sugar cookies," she said over her shoulder. "The children are very excited about welcoming you."

I followed her past the parlor, through the dining room, and into the kitchen, where Gabe and Gilly sat waiting at a long kitchen table. They looked up at me with sugar-coated grins.

Mrs. Wilder laughed. "They've been sampling, as you can see."

I laughed, too. I'd never expected such a greeting.

"Gabriel, Gillian, this is Mercy Kaplan. She'll be helping out just the way Vera did."

The kids waved, and Gilly pointed a chubby finger at the plate of cookies. "We made lots. Want some?" she asked.

"Why, yes, I would; thank you very much." I draped my coat over a chair and sat across from them. Gabe pushed the plate toward me, and they waited, watching while I took my first bite.

"Oh my!" I said, eyes wide with pretended surprise. "I don't think I've ever tasted a better cookie!"

They giggled, and the sweet, familiar sound rushed through me, swelling like the creek after a spring rain, cascading into the deep, silent well that had opened up the day I left Mama and the kids to go to the Bonners. Their eyes shone with that easy trust that Justice and Honor always had, and I finally knew. I needed these fatherless children even more than they needed me.

I swallowed hard and tried to keep smiling. They'd be easy to love, no doubt, but I was already dreading the time when I'd have to leave them. And it would come. Nothing was forever.

"Now, you two stay here," Mrs. Wilder told the kids, "while I show Mercy the rest of the house."

"Yes, ma'am," Gabe said.

Gilly gave me a shy grin and wiggled her fingers in a good-bye wave.

Upstairs, Mrs. Wilder showed me the four bedrooms one by one. Beds were neatly made in each, chests and dressers sat dust-free and shiny, but various drawers had been pulled out, emptied onto the floor. Trunks at the foot of every bed were open, their contents tossed about.

Mrs. Wilder became more disturbed with each room, her face a canvas of growing anxiety, till at last she leaned close and whispered low in my ear, "I looked everywhere, M, but I couldn't find it. You *will* help me find it, won't you?"

I stared at her, unsure of what to say. Had she called me M—M for "Mercy"?

"Yes, of course, Mrs. Wilder." I tried to sound as if everyone called me M. "I'd be happy to help. What did you lose?"

She raised a blank face to me, blinked several times, then turned toward the stairs.

"You must see your room," she said. "It's small and just off the kitchen, but it's airy and bright."

Confusion flickered through me.

"I think you'll find it quite comfortable," she said. "Warm in the winter and cool in the summer."

"Um . . . thank you, Mrs. Wilder. I'm . . . I'm sure I will."

"Vera always seemed pleased with it," she added.

I followed her back to the kitchen, full of questions about what had just happened, but when Gabe and Gilly looked up at me with their sugar-smeared grins, I forgot all my doubts.

What did it matter that Mrs. Wilder's mind wandered?

"All things must change
To something new, to something strange."
HENRY WADSWORTH LONGFELLOW

MY ROOM WAS SMALL, but it was everything Mrs. Wilder had said and more. A lace-trimmed comforter lay on the bed, and sunlight streamed through big windows dressed in ruffled swag curtains. I'd never slept in a room so nice. I stood there staring till Mrs. Wilder's voice shook me from my stupor.

"It's a pretty little room, don't you think?" she asked, pushing her hand deep into her apron pocket. She fingered something inside, moving it this way and that, and the corner of an envelope peeked out.

I smiled at her. "Yes, it's very pretty, Mrs. Wilder. Thank you."

She shoved the letter down safe inside, yanked out her hand, and began discussing what I might prepare for dinner tonight and how she wanted me to join them for meals just as Vera had done.

"I think it's important to maintain a sense of family for the children," she said. "I'd also like you to tutor them in learning their numbers and letters—at the kitchen table, please, not in their room."

"Yes, ma'am."

"It's something Father wanted—"

She squeezed her eyes shut and shook her head. "I meant to say, it's something *Mr. Wilder* wanted, but . . ."

Her gaze fell to the floor in front of us.

". . . but now . . ."

Her voice trailed off again, making me think that mentioning her husband had brought back the awful memory of his loss, but that wasn't it at all. Something else had caught her attention, and her eyes were fixed on the floor at her feet.

"I'll be happy to work with the children, Mrs. Wilder."

I waited, but she didn't answer.

"Would midmorning be okay? After the morning chores?"

She bent, picked up a large black button, and without a word headed for the stairs.

I DIDN'T QUITE know what to think of my new employer, but taking over the kitchen and cleaning up after the kids felt as natural as breathing, especially with Mrs. Wilder staying in her room most of the time. The children were well mannered and appeared happy just to sit at the table, watching me prepare a hen for stewing.

"You gonna make dumplings with that chicken?" Gabe asked, looking far too serious to be talking about supper.

I nodded and pulled out a large pot. "Do you like dumplings?"

"Yeah, but Daddy liked 'em better'n anybody."

"He's way up in the sky now," Gilly said in that baby voice of hers, "with the angels."

I wasn't sure what to say. I set the pot on the stove and turned around. "Maybe your daddy will see my mama there."

Gabe looked up at me, thoughtful like. "Your mama's in heaven, too?"

I nodded.

"Do you think your mama and my daddy might be friends?" he asked.

"I don't know, but I'm sure she'd like it if they were."

He nodded real slow. "I bet my daddy would, too."

"You gonna be our friend now?" Gilly asked.

Choking back tears, I knelt and slipped my arms around their small shoulders. "Yes," I whispered. "I would like that most of all."

THAT EVENING, while I set the table, I saw Daniel swing around the corner of the house on his crutches, headed for the kitchen door. He picked up the soap and washbowl by the back step, filled the bowl from the rain barrel, and began scrubbing away the black grease that covered his hands and arms.

I thought again about that dark night when Gabe was lost and the unexpected confusion Daniel had stirred in me. I had to admit that it had scared me at first. But now, as I watched him through the kitchen window, I felt more in control. There'd be no more butterflies. I'd make sure of that. I was here to cook, clean, and take care of the kids. That was all.

When he finished and made his way through the door, I handed him a kitchen towel. He nodded his thanks but eyed me closely as he dried off.

"How were things today?" he asked.

"Very good."

He tossed me a skeptical look and glanced upstairs. "No problems?"

"Not at all. In fact, the kids were very well behaved." I pulled a pitcher of milk from the icebox. "We'll be ready to eat soon. Shall I send Gabe to tell his mother?"

He shook his head. "I'll do it." He leaned one crutch against the wall, and with the aid of the handrail worked his way up the back stairs with surprising ease. His leg appeared to be healing well.

Daniel didn't seem as open and friendly as Owen or Garrett, but he was a far cry from Mrs. Wilder, which was a blessing. Otherwise, I might've felt as if I'd fallen into a rabbit hole like the one in *Alice's Adventures in Wonderland*.

I was glad Beth had told me how seriously Daniel took his responsibilities. Still, I'd sensed something of Mr. Bonner in him, like he peered at the world from behind a wall. I had to wonder if it was the painful loss of his father that had put him there. If so, that wasn't so hard to understand. I knew what it was like to lose a parent. I'd lost my whole family. When I found the graves that first night, I'd even let myself wish that I'd been taken by the influenza, too, but surely Daniel hadn't been so weak. Unlike his stepmother, he'd seemed to have far too much fight in him the night Gabe was lost, far too much determination, to wish for anything so selfish and foolish. He and his stepmother were a puzzle, though. It might be best to do what was expected of me and just stay out of their way.

We soon gathered around the table, Mrs. Wilder in her black dress at one end and an empty chair at the other. Daniel took a seat by Gabe, and I chose a chair across from them, next to Gilly.

Gabe stole glances at the head of the table as though he expected his father to appear there—if not this time, maybe the next—and my heart ached for him. I'm sure Daniel noticed, too. He reached for the boy's hand under the table.

"Daniel," Mrs. Wilder said, "would you say grace, please?"

"Yes, ma'am." He bowed his head and gave a brief, humble blessing.

"You forgot something," Gabe said with a frown.

Daniel nodded and bowed his head again. "And, Lord, please watch over our father."

"'Member hugs and kisses, Daniel," Gilly said. "Big ones."

Daniel squirmed. "Okay, okay. *And* send him hugs and kisses, big ones, from Gabe and Gilly."

"From you, too," she said.

"Yes, from me, too. Now, say amen, okay?"

The kids did as they were told, then sat back, satisfied at last, but a pink flush had brightened Daniel's face. I tried hard not to smile. Apparently, he didn't enjoy feeling so exposed, but I found his reaction interesting. Maybe I'd been too hasty in my first opinion of him that night Gabe was lost. His stepmother was strange, no doubt, but in the last few moments, I'd seen Daniel try to make up for that, like he had to find ways to bridge the gulf his father had left behind, ways to keep his memory alive and make things feel normal, even if it embarrassed him.

After dinner, Mrs. Wilder sent me upstairs to get the kids ready for bed. "You've had a long first day," she said. "Daniel and I will clean up here, and you can read the children their Bible story."

I thanked her, said good night, and herded Gabe and Gilly upstairs.

The nursery held two small beds with pictures of angels hanging above them. Since my morning glance through the upstairs rooms with Mrs. Wilder, scattered clothing had been neatly folded, and drawers had been put back in place. Maybe she'd found what she'd been looking for.

I helped the kids change into their nightclothes, and they crawled into bed without a fuss. They'd had a long day, too. It couldn't have been easy for them to lose Vera and welcome someone new into their lives so quickly. I pulled out their Bible stories, but their eyes had already clouded with sleep. Before David could bring down Goliath, they were both breathing deeply.

I sat by their bedsides a moment, watching them sleep, studying their soft round faces, their pink cheeks, and felt an unexpected panic building in me. Two and a half months had passed since I'd last seen my family, and suddenly I couldn't quite remember Justice's laugh. Or Honor's tiny fingers. Or even the way Charity lit up when she talked about her writing. I squeezed my eyes shut, praying that these small memories wouldn't be whisked away, too, and after what seemed like a frightfully long time, a picture of them took shape in my head. With relief, I saw them all, just the way they looked the last night Papa played his harmonica for us.

Breathing easier, I checked the kids again, tucked their quilts around them, and headed downstairs. When I passed through the kitchen on my way to my room, not a dish was out of place. Mrs. Wilder and Daniel must've finished quickly and gone to bed. My first day was done.

I changed into my nightgown and stood at the window, shivering in the dark. An orange moon hung low in the winter sky, looking far too weighty to do anything more than just laze on the shadowy horizon. My thoughts shifted to home again, bringing me a fleeting picture of moonlight on graves. With a shudder, I shook the image away, pulled back the lacy coverlet on my bed, and climbed in, hoping that the newness of this day might overpower the pain that always crept into my heart at night.

The sheets smelled of winter winds, and I breathed in the sweetness. With gratitude, I felt myself slipping away. But, please, I asked, no dreams. Not tonight.

Just . . . sleep.

SOMETHING WOKE ME.

I looked around the room but saw nothing unusual. I glanced out the window. I'd been asleep for a while. The heavy moon had managed to rise bright and high in the crisp, cold sky.

I relaxed, but not for long. A light rapping brought me quickly to my feet. Maybe a knock was what had awakened me to start with. I hurried to the door, turned the knob, and peered through the crack. "Yes?"

"M, it's me! Let me in."

Startled, I opened the door, thinking of the night Gabe disappeared, and Mrs. Wilder scurried inside.

"Is something wrong?" I asked. "Are the kids okay?"

She clutched a crumpled envelope in her fist. "It's this . . . this *thing*." She waved it in my face. "I've had it since yesterday, but I just couldn't bring myself to open it."

"What is it?" I asked.

"He's coming, M. He's coming, and there's nothing we can do about it!"

"Please, Mrs. Wilder, sit down." I led her to the bed.

"He can't find out," she whispered.

"Find out what, Mrs. Wilder? Who's coming?"

She turned her face toward the bright moonlight, and I saw her stifling fear slide to cool composure, like rain-laden clouds parting to reveal blue sky.

"Mercy, I'm . . . I'm so sorry I woke you." Her hand relaxed, and the twisted letter fell to the floor. "Are you warm enough?"

I couldn't answer.

She patted me on the knee. "Remember there are extra quilts in the closet if you need them."

She rose and slipped down the hall while I sat there in shocked silence.

chapter
21

I STARED AT the crumpled envelope on the floor, and for a moment, I was tempted to open it, but only for a moment. I felt Mama close by, ready to fuss, and quickly decided that I had to return it to Mrs. Wilder, unread.

I picked up the letter and smoothed the wrinkles, worried that its return might cause more distress. Mrs. Wilder probably wouldn't sleep a wink if I brought it back to her tonight. I made a quick decision and laid the envelope on my night table. I'd make sure she got it first thing tomorrow.

The next morning, I dressed early, made my bed, and placed the letter in the center of the kitchen table. The kids came down as soon as they smelled the bacon cooking and sat watching while I pulled biscuits from the oven. Their eyes glittered with expectation, but it wasn't from hunger.

"Mama said you're going to teach us our numbers and ABCs," Gabe said.

I nodded. "I surely am. We'll start right after the chores are done."

"I can help," Gilly said.

"Yeah, me, too," Gabe agreed. "You'll get done real fast if *we* help."

I pulled the butter dish from the icebox and set it on the table, near the letter. "I'm sure I will. After all, you two are pretty big already. I bet there are lots of things you can do."

They gave me appreciative grins; then Gilly hollered, "Mama!"

Mrs. Wilder stepped into the room from the back stairs and slipped her arms around the kids. "Mmmm," she murmured. "Something smells good."

"Mercy's making breakfast," Gabe said. "I'm hungry; are you, Mama?"

"Starving." She looked around the kitchen. "Is there anything I can do to help?" she asked.

"No, ma'am, except tell me how you like your eggs."

"Oh, no eggs for me." She went to the cupboard and pulled out a big jar of plum jam. "I'll just have one of those big lovely biscuits."

"Me, too!" Gilly shouted.

"Well," Gabe said, "maybe I'll have just one egg."

I grinned at him and pulled out the skillet.

I fried Gabe's egg over easy, the way he asked me to, and just as I wondered if Daniel would be joining us, he came thumping down the stairs. I had no idea a person with a broken leg could move so fast.

"Gotta get going," he said, tucking biscuits and bacon into

a napkin. "Promised to get the Hollomans' Model T finished today." He poked an extra strip of bacon into his mouth, gripped his crutches, and muttered, "Mmm, good," before he headed out the door.

Mrs. Wilder went back upstairs as soon as she finished her breakfast, but it wasn't till I cleared the table that I noticed the letter was gone, too. I was pleased it hadn't disturbed her, but I was a bit disappointed that I hadn't had a chance to find out who was coming, or why she'd been so upset by the prospect of an unexpected visit.

When the kitchen was clean again, I went to work on the rest of the house, making beds, sweeping floors, and dusting everywhere but Mrs. Wilder's room. She said she'd take care of that herself.

The kids scampered around like puppies, undoing much of what I accomplished. As I figured, with all their extra help, I had only a half-hour to spend on their studies before cooking the noon meal. It would be time enough, though, as small as they were. Justice could never sit still for long, either.

Gabe gathered pencils and paper from the desk and brought them to the kitchen table. I made a practice page for him, and while he copied lines of numbers, Gilly and I practiced counting chairs and cups and spoons.

Before the half-hour was up, Mrs. Wilder walked into the kitchen. Her face looked as flushed and frantic as it had last night in the moonlight. I stood, wondering if she'd call me M again, but she only flapped her hands nervously at the kids and asked them to go to their room. They gave her a look that said they'd seen this sort of thing many times before and scurried up the stairs. Their mother's fluttering hand settled over her heart.

"Please sit down, Mercy," she said in a breathy voice.

I took my seat while she tried to compose herself.

"I've had news from my father recently," she said. "He will arrive here for a holiday visit next Tuesday."

I did a quick calculation. "Christmas Eve?" I asked.

"Yes, Christmas Eve. We'll need to dust the spare bedroom and change the bedding. Father always expects fresh bedding."

I nodded. "I'll take care of that right before he's due. Will we prepare a special meal for his arrival, too?"

Mrs. Wilder's fragile composure slipped for a moment, and her hands twisted in her skirts.

"Yes, of course. We must discuss the meals. Father likes stuffed hens for Christmas Eve. And ham on Christmas Day." She gave me a worried frown. "Oh, but, Mercy, Christmas Day is Wednesday, your day off."

I had hoped to spend that day with Emma and Beth, but Mrs. Wilder looked so panic-stricken.

"Please don't worry," I said with as much reassurance as I could. "I'll stay Christmas morning. We can get it all done."

She sighed deeply and managed a smile. "I promise not to make you work all day. Just long enough to see me through the worst of the preparation. Oh, and you must stay for dinner."

"Thank you, but if you don't mind, I'd like to visit friends once the meal is in the oven."

"Yes. Yes, of course you would." She reached for my hand across the table and gave it a squeeze. "Thank you, Mercy," she said. "We'll have a lovely meal, and it will be just the way he likes it. And . . . and everything will be fine now, won't it?"

I gave her a confident nod, but I wasn't at all convinced.

MRS. WILDER DIDN'T come downstairs to eat her noon meal. After I fed the children and settled them down for an afternoon nap, I prepared a tray for her and took it upstairs. I found her door ajar, and as I approached the room, I glimpsed her pacing around a small writing table. I really didn't mean to spy on her, but what I witnessed kept me riveted outside the door. Even Mama wouldn't have been able to pull me away.

On the lace-covered table lay the large black button I'd seen Mrs. Wilder pick up from the floor yesterday. She pointed an accusing finger at it, her eyes squinted in anger, then paced again, muttering to herself. She went back to pick up the button, and even from the doorway I could hear her breath quicken. Her chest rose and fell with great swallows of air, and her whole body seemed to tremble. She slapped the button back on the table, let out a stifled sob, and dropped, facedown, onto the bed.

My hands shook, and dishes rattled. Mrs. Wilder shot a startled look toward the door, then ran to me.

"Oh, M," she whispered, pulling me inside, "I'm so glad you're here." She wiped her tears and waved a hand toward the

146

button. "I don't want to think about all those bad things anymore." Her face lit up. "Let's get away, go for a picnic by the creek. The grass is tall and green, and deer will be grazing everywhere. Remember how it was last time?"

I couldn't speak. Green grass at this time of year? Remember last time?

"Here," she said, running back to the table. "I'll get rid of this awful thing, and we'll never think of it again." She flung the button across the room, where it hit the wall and clattered to the floor. "Now he'll never know what I did," she whispered.

I didn't know what to do, what to say, but when she turned to me with such expectation, I knew I had to think of something.

"Look what I've brought you," I said, remembering the tray. I set it on the table. "Ham and potatoes, and more biscuits, too, with some of that plum jam you like."

"But, M, we can't stay. You know I can't be here when Father gets home. What if he already knows?" Her lower lip quivered. "Oh, M," she moaned, "I should've been braver. I should've never done what I did."

Her frightened words tumbled in my head. What horrible thing had she done?

"Please," I said finally. "Just eat a little. Maybe we can get away when you're finished, okay?"

She pouted like a small child while I just stood there, trying to be what she needed.

With a brooding reluctance, she finally picked up her fork. Thankful, I slipped away, easing the door shut behind me.

MRS. WILDER DIDN'T come down again that evening, and by suppertime, I'd decided that I had to know more about her. I had to know what terrible deed haunted her so much that she forgot who I was and slipped into another season, another age. But mostly I had to know for the children's sake. Did she forget them, too, during those strange lapses?

But who would tell me more? Emma certainly didn't seem willing, and Daniel didn't strike me as one to discuss family affairs, especially with hired help. Yet I had to ask. I was worried about leaving Gabe and Gilly alone with their mother on my days off.

I glanced out the kitchen window and saw Daniel washing up. While he swung through the doorway on his crutches, I reached for a towel and waited, hoping I might ask a few questions before everyone came down to dinner.

Like yesterday, he accepted the towel with a nod of thanks, then asked how my day went.

"The kids were good, as always," I told him, "but . . ." I glanced up the back stairs.

"There's been a problem." He stated his conclusion simply, as if he'd expected it all along.

"Well, yes," I said. "At least I think so."

"Cora?"

"It's just that she said some odd things, and I really don't know what to do."

He nodded. "No one does."

Mrs. Wilder stepped onto the upstairs landing. "Is dinner almost ready?" she asked.

"Yes, ma'am. Shall I fetch the children for you?"

"No, thank you. I'll get them."

She turned back to the hallway, looking every bit as whole and alert as she did the first day I saw her in Mr. Hilliard's store.

For a moment, Daniel didn't say anything. He gave me a narrow, discerning look, and then, in an abrupt move, he leaned close and whispered, "Tonight on the back porch, after everyone goes to bed."

Before I could answer, footsteps thudded down the upstairs hall. "Daniel!" Gilly called from the landing. She and Gabe hurried down, all grins, to welcome their brother home. He gave them hugs and helped them wash up for supper.

I didn't have much time to think about Daniel's command to meet him later, but I felt a niggling worry in the pit of my stomach. After all, proper girls weren't supposed to meet alone with boys they didn't know, especially at that hour. I waited for Mama to fuss, but she was quiet.

Getting through supper was difficult, but even more so was waiting for everyone to go to bed. I left my door ajar, listening for Daniel to come through the kitchen, and when I heard the soft creak of floorboards, my stomach gave a fierce flutter. I reached for my coat and stood there while my anger flared. I'd already been betrayed by my thoughts that night Gabe was lost.

149

I wasn't about to let it happen again. I focused my attention on the children, determined to keep my wits about me, and slipped out to join Daniel on the steps.

"We won't be overheard here," he whispered.

The orange moon rose full and round again, half hidden behind tall cedars. Daniel sat on one end of the step, and I sat beside him, leaving a respectable space between us. I was here to help the children, Cora, too, and I surely didn't want him to think anything else.

For a while he was quiet, so I let him be, hoping he wasn't here to tell me that I should stay out of his family affairs. I guess he was only thinking of his recent loss, though, because he asked, "Do you have a father?"

His question caught me off guard, and for a moment, I couldn't seem to switch my thoughts from his family to mine. Then Papa's face came to me. I saw his eyes and felt his arms around me. I saw the bedroll strapped to his back and the sad slope of his shoulders as he headed down the road, away from his home and family.

A sick misery washed over me. "I can't be sure," I said finally.

Even in the dim moonlight I could see the confusion in his face. There was no escape. I'd have to explain. I reached inside me and pulled up the barest of details, flinching as each barbed word cut its way out of me.

"My papa left to find work when our cotton crop failed," I told him. "I'm sure he would've written if he could've, but there's been no word for a very long time. I fear he may have been taken by the influenza, like your daddy."

I swallowed hard, blinked away tears, and saw Daniel lean toward me in obvious sympathy. For a moment, I feared he might reach for my hand, but he pulled away again. "What about your mother?" he asked. "Do you have brothers or sisters?"

I braced myself for more sharp barbs. "They're gone, too. Mama and Charity, Justice and Honor, all lost to the influenza."

There. I was finally done. Now he knew.

"Your whole family?" He looked stunned. "I'm . . . I'm sorry." He sounded breathy and flustered. "I didn't know."

The pain in his eyes shoved me over the edge. I was sinking. I pulled in a desperate breath and pushed him back toward his own family. "But you lost both your parents, too, right?"

"Yeah, but I don't remember much about my mother. She died when I was four, and Father married Cora when I was thirteen."

"That must've been so hard for you, starting over like that."

He gave me a slow shake of his head. "Oh, Mercy, not nearly as rough as what you're going through. Not nearly."

I saw amazement light his eyes, but it was the tenderness behind his words that rushed through me without warning. It flowed from him, easy and genuine, and before I knew it, I'd let it wash over the parched fields inside me, let it pull me closer to tears all over again.

"No," Daniel went on, "starting over wasn't too bad at first."

I centered my thoughts on the kids again, and listened closely.

"Cora had lapses even in the beginning, like the night Gabe was lost, but Father always seemed to know what to do to ease her through them. Then Gabe and Gilly were born only a year and a half apart. They've dealt with this craziness all their lives, and now . . . well, losing Father has been difficult for them."

I nodded slowly, nervous about asking anything more of him, but there was so much I needed to know. "I've often wondered," I said, deciding to risk his irritation, "what happened the night Gabe was lost, how he ended up in the cold the way he did."

He huffed his frustration, making me fear I'd pushed too hard, but I soon realized his annoyance wasn't aimed at me.

"I know it sounds crazy—it does even to me—but Gabe insists his mother got him up to play hide-and-seek."

I stared at him. "And you believe him?"

He nodded slowly. "I do."

I thought about how Mrs. Wilder had pleaded to go on a picnic this afternoon, to sit in the tall green grass and watch deer grazing, and I had to wonder if her lapse with Gabe had been like that. I pulled my coat tighter around me. This was certainly no weather for games and picnics.

"Things have worsened since Father died," Daniel said. "I tried to reassure her, told her I'd stay and help with the expenses and the kids, but I guess she felt like she'd lost the only person who could keep her safe."

"Safe from what?"

"I'm not sure. Her father, maybe. Cyrus Collier seemed nice enough the one time I met him, but something about him sure made me uneasy."

"No heart signs?"

Daniel blinked. "What?"

"It's just something my mama taught me. She said to watch for heart signs, that they'd show you what's right and good in a person, even when you don't think it's there."

"Well, I sure didn't see any signs with Mr. Collier. Father didn't seem to care for him much, either." Daniel gave the moon a thoughtful look. "I think he didn't like that Cora was afraid of the man."

"But why? Because he was strict?" I peered up at him. "Or could it have been something she did when she was young, something bad that kept her from facing him?"

He turned to look at me. "Something bad?"

I cringed. "Maybe. I don't know; it's just that Mrs. Wilder said some really strange things today that made me wonder."

"Like what?"

"She said she should've never done what she did and that she was afraid her father might find out. She called me M and asked me to go on a picnic with her so she'd be gone when her father got home."

"She called you Em? That's what she calls Mrs. Sayers, down at the Glory. Em for Emma."

I finally understood. I touched my braid. "I guess I do look a bit like her with my hair done this way."

He'd solved one puzzle, but there was much more I wanted to understand. "Did you know that Emma worked for the Colliers years ago, when she and Mrs. Wilder were still girls?" I asked.

"Yeah, I did. I think she and Cora were almost like sisters."

"And would you know anything about a black button?" I asked.

He nodded. "I've seen it. Sometimes she loses it and turns the whole house upside down trying to find it."

"You don't know why?"

"Father might've known, but he never told me. Why?"

"It seems to upset her so—that button and the letter she got from her father."

"Letter?"

"He'll be arriving Tuesday for a Christmas visit."

Daniel's head jerked up. "For how long?"

"She didn't say. Is it a problem?"

"Well, he's not the kind of man to make social visits, even to family. It's been at least four years since we last saw him. He wanted to see the land and the house, and Gabe, of course, his first grandson."

"Do you think he wants something?"

"Could be he wants the property Father left to Cora. I was given the repair shop and the parcel close to the creek, but the rest went to Cora. With the kids so small, Father wanted to make sure they'd always have a home."

"But I thought Mr. Collier was a wealthy man. Why would he want it?"

Daniel shrugged. "I guess men like that never stop wanting more."

I had no experience with that kind of power or money, but I couldn't fathom why any man would steal from his own daughter, especially when he had so much already. I glanced at Daniel. "How can we help her?"

He shook his head. "We might never find a way, but it's Gabe and Gilly I worry about most. They're so young. They don't understand any of this." He threw up his hands. "I don't understand it, either!"

I glimpsed a shadow of fear in his face, reminding me of the way he looked that first time I saw him, sitting by the garden shed, shivering in the cold, his coat wrapped around Gabe. He'd looked scared but determined, like there was nothing he wouldn't do for his little brother.

"I'll be here every day but Wednesday," I told him, "and I can be here then, too, if you need me. With both of us watching out for the kids, we can keep them safe."

He turned his face to mine, and the rising moon lit a puzzled smile.

"You don't even know us, Mercy. Why do you care?"

I stared past the shadowy trees, right into the old cabin, and saw Justice prancing across the floor on his stick horse while Honor watched, almost breathless from a flood of giggles.

Why did I care? Because of the kids, of course. The kids.

Again tears stung, but I turned to Daniel anyway. "There's nothing I can do for my own family anymore. But maybe I can do something for Gabe and Gilly."

He nodded slowly, then rose to his feet. He reached to help me up, and I slid my hand in his, easily and without hesitation. Realizing too late what I'd done, I backed away, embarrassed, only to see him cross the space between us, despite my discomfort, and lean close.

"I'm glad you're here," he whispered.

chapter 23

I WOKE THE NEXT morning feeling restless, eager, like something exceptional might be coming my way. It was a delicious feeling, one I hadn't felt in a very long time. For a moment, I let myself bask in it, but I soon had to question where it came from. I stared at the ceiling, trying to remember.

Ah yes, today was my day off. I planned to spend the whole day at the Glory, if Daniel could spare me.

Daniel.

My stomach pitched. I felt him lean close all over again, felt his breath on my cheek, and heard him whisper, "I'm glad . . ."

I squeezed my eyes shut and threw back the covers.

How weak-willed and stupid could a girl be, anyway? Daniel wasn't what I wanted at all, and even if I did, it would be a hopeless situation with Mrs. Wilder the way she was. I'd end up worse off than Mama ever thought about being, caring for a crazy woman the rest of my life.

I jumped out of bed, washed up, and braided my hair. Just outside the door, I bumped into Daniel.

He laughed, easy like and a bit too familiar. "I was just

coming to get you. I'm making breakfast for Gabe and Gilly and thought you'd like something to eat before you leave."

His smiling green eyes made me flinch. I backed away. "Thank you, but no," I murmured. "I'll just be on my way, if that's okay."

"Sure." His smile faded, and he turned back to the stove. "I can take care of the kids all day today."

I nodded, thankful. "But if a time comes when you can't miss work on my day off, don't hesitate to tell me. I won't mind staying with them."

"I appreciate that."

I slipped into my coat. "I'll . . . um . . . see you late tonight, perhaps."

"Late?"

"Well, yes. I wanted to help Emma at the Glory and have supper with her after closing, if that's okay."

"Yes, of course. It's your day."

"Thank you." I raised a hand in goodbye and headed for the door.

Outside, the rising sun had sent its warmth sailing across the frosted brown grass, leaving wet diamonds sparkling in its wake. It felt good to be out of the house for a while, away from the mystery surrounding Mrs. Wilder, away from . . .

There he was again. Right there in my head. I dragged my thoughts from Daniel, pushed them hard toward the Glory, and refused to look back.

The dining room was probably filling up with hungry

townspeople this very moment. Emma and Beth would be taking orders, flipping pancakes, frying eggs and potatoes. Suddenly I was hungry for one of Emma's big biscuits with sausage gravy, so I picked up my step, looking forward to being in her warm kitchen once again.

I slipped around back and knocked on the screen. "Can you use a little help?" I asked.

"Beth, look who's here!" Emma jerked open the door and pulled me inside. "We sure didn't 'spect to see you so soon," she said, grinning.

Beth stood by the stove, frying ham, her face crinkled with curiosity. She raised a hand to wave hello.

"How's it goin' over there?" Emma asked.

"Good. The kids are no trouble at all, and the house is beautiful and easy to clean."

She gave me a piercing look, as if she expected more, but I had no intention of discussing the Wilders in front of Beth. The rest would have to wait.

"You should see my room, Emma," I said, keeping the conversation light. "It's the nicest I've ever slept in."

"Then you're happy with the position?"

I nodded.

"Good." She pulled an apron off a hook on the storeroom door and slipped it over my head. "If you're so determined to cook on your only day off," she said, tying it around my waist, "then the least we can do is try to send you home clean."

"And full, I hope. I was thinking about your biscuits and gravy all the way over here."

Emma laughed and headed for the dining room with a tray full of pancakes. "Help yourself."

THE DAY SLID from one meal into another till at last Beth headed upstairs with her supper tray. Emma and I sat at the kitchen table with crusty bread and bowls of stew, eating and laughing about the day's dining-room gossip till Emma could take no more.

She rested her elbows on the table and leaned toward me. "Now, I *know* somethin' musta brung you here besides my biscuits and gravy. What was it?"

She'd probably known all along I had questions about the Wilders. I smiled and shrugged. "Won't do much good to ask if you don't plan to answer."

She gave me a suspicious look. "I'll answer what I can."

"Fair enough." I looked her in the eye. "I need to know why Mrs. Wilder is the way she is."

Emma leaned back in her chair. "That's a tall order, Mercy. I'm not sure I can answer all of that one for you, but I can tell you she wasn't always that way."

"When did she change?"

Something in the way Emma cocked her head made me think she might never tell the whole story, but I waited anyway, eager to hear what I could.

"It happened after Cora lost her mother," she said.

"Beth mentioned that. The woman was trampled by horses, right?"

Emma gave me a cynical glance but didn't answer.

"Were you living there then?"

She pushed her stew bowl back and reached for her coffee mug. "Yeah, I was there. I was thirteen when I first came to live with the Colliers. My mama died years before, and I guess Daddy finally decided I was too much of a burden to stay on with him and my brother, Joe. They took off and left me with the Colliers to work for my keep. I never saw either of 'em again."

"You mean they just up and left you?" I couldn't imagine a father doing something like that on purpose, not to his own daughter.

She nodded. "It was hard at first, but Mrs. Collier was good to me, and I had Cora. She was twelve, just a year younger, and we got along like sisters, somethin' her father couldn't abide. After all, I wasn't even hired help. I was just a charity case nobody wanted 'ceptin' his wife."

I waited while she took a sip of coffee.

"They were scared of that man, you know—all of 'em. I was, too, but I guess seeing the way he expected everyone to jump to attention ever' time he entered a room made me stubborn enough to stand up to him. Not brave enough to disobey, mind you, but, oh, I swore he'd never see me scared." She let out a contemptuous snicker. "I think that's what got his goat the most—that and the way Cora's older brother watched me all the time."

"Devon?"

I raised an eyebrow, and she pointed her finger at me. "Now, you need to know none of that was my doin'. The old man brought all that misery on hisself. The more he talked bad about me, the more Devon was determined to prove him wrong, no matter how many straps got laid across his backside. I guess the man was scared I might ruin his boy's chances of marryin' high and mighty one day." She grinned. "And I guess I did."

"What do you mean?"

The easy grin soured, and her eyes turned dark. She pushed back her chair, and for a moment I thought she'd had enough of old memories. With relief, I watched her refill her coffee cup and sit back down.

"Devon wanted me to run off and marry him," she said. "I loved him, so I did."

I stared at her, dumbfounded. "So Beth—"

"Beth's a Collier."

"But your last name is Sayers."

"Made it up before I moved back. Just seemed easier that way."

"So Beth doesn't know?"

Emma shook her head. "Only Cora and her father know. And now you."

"What happened to Devon?"

"He died a week after we married, not long after his mother's death."

I watched that old sorrow sweep across her face like a winter wind. She shuddered, and when she looked up again, I saw the pain in her eyes, glistening like ice.

"I wasn't with him when it happened," she said, "but I was told he was trampled by a horse and wagon, like his mama."

"Oh, Emma," I whispered. "I'm sorry. But . . . but isn't it kinda strange they both died the same way?"

She shrugged. "It's been a long time since it happened, almost fifteen years, and a long time since I let myself think about it. Cora ain't never been the same since." She shook her head. "None of this rehashin' can help her, Mercy. It's just bad ol' stuff, not fit to mention anymore. What's done is done."

She pushed back her chair, seemingly finished, but I grabbed her arm.

"Emma," I pleaded, "there has to be more you can tell me. Daniel said it was Mrs. Wilder who took Gabe from his bed that night—his own mother—to play hide-and-seek out in the cold, and then she just left him out there. Did you know that?"

Emma took another sip of her coffee.

"And the woman talks to me like I'm you. She calls me Em and acts like we're great friends, planning picnics and playing games. And now"—I threw up my hands—"now she's near crazy over a letter from Mr. Collier and this silly black button that keeps her scared to death her father is going to find out about some horrible thing she did."

"A letter?" Emma stared at me, eyes narrow and suspicious.

I nodded. "He wrote to say he's coming for a visit."

"When?"

"Christmas Eve."

Her face twisted, mirroring a hundred unvoiced words, and though there was no way I could cipher all I'd glimpsed, I'd seen enough to be worried.

chapter
24

THE MOON FLOATED high in the sky by the time I got home, but, late as it was, embers still glowed in the fireplace. I found my bedroom door pushed open to receive the last of the warmth and couldn't help but wonder who'd been thinking of me, Mrs. Wilder or Daniel.

My fingers trembled as I pulled off my clothes, but I knew it wasn't from just the cold. I was neck-deep in whatever had twisted Mrs. Wilder's mind, and Emma seemed to have only some of the answers. She wasn't shocked by anything I'd told her—not the childish way Mrs. Wilder played games or called me Em, or even the way she obsessed over a black button. Nothing surprised Emma at all till I mentioned that letter.

I couldn't stop thinking about yesterday, about how scared Mrs. Wilder was of being found out by her father. Emma had offered no explanation for that, either. Yet, short of murder, what could a young girl have done that would've been so terrible?

I pulled on my gown, but just before I slid under the covers, I heard a light rap at the door. I groaned.

Please. Not Mrs. Wilder again. Not tonight. I eased the

door open a crack and found myself almost nose to nose with Daniel.

"Can we talk?" he asked.

After last night, I wasn't so sure. I'd let something happen, something I didn't want to happen, and I didn't quite understand why. It seemed I couldn't trust myself anymore. "I'm sorry," I told him. "It's very late. Are the kids okay?"

"Yes, but, please, Mercy, I won't keep you long."

I studied his face. He looked worried, too worried to be coaxing me back out to the porch without good reason. I finally nodded and reached for my coat.

Outside, clouds had rolled in, hiding the moon and stars. I stepped carefully across the dark porch, feeling for the edge with my foot, and saw Daniel raise a shadowy arm toward me.

"Here, take my hand," he whispered.

I felt for the post, not wanting to repeat last night's mistake. "I'm okay," I said, easing onto the step. "Did something happen today?"

I could barely see him nod.

"I kept thinking about last night, about the way Cora called you Em and talked to you like you were Mrs. Sayers."

He turned toward me, shoes scraping over the step, and his knee brushed mine. I scooted away, determined to put a more respectable distance between us, but not even a firm hand pressed against my belly could stop the startled butterflies.

"You already know how worried I am about Gabe and Gilly."

"Yes, of course," I said, focusing again on the kids.

"We need to know what happened to Cora, right? It might be the only way we can keep her from doing something crazy with the kids again."

I nodded. "So what did you do? Did you find out something?"

He blew out a long breath. He seemed reluctant to tell me, then just blurted it out. "I wore Father's coat and boots today."

"Oh, Daniel," I whispered, "that must've been so hard on her."

"I know."

I heard his voice tremble and was glad I couldn't see his eyes. "What happened?"

"She was startled at first but didn't say anything. As the day wore on, she seemed to adjust to the idea that it was only natural I should make use of my father's clothing, but tonight all that changed."

Daniel's breath quickened. "I turned out the lights, and while I was banking the fire, she came up behind me. I guess she took me for Father. She said, 'Can you ever forgive me, Samuel, for laying such unrelenting trouble at your feet?'"

I sucked in a breath. "Daniel, your father *knew*—he knew what she did. What did you say to her?"

"I didn't know what to say. I finally had to turn around and face her, and when I did, she just gave me a dazed look and thanked me for taking care of the fire."

"Nothing more?"

"That's it."

I sat there, imagining how terrible this must've been for

her—for him, too. But why would she need her husband's forgiveness? Unless . . .

"Do you know about her mother and brother?" I asked.

"Sure. They died a long time ago. Everyone knows that."

"Emma said they both died the same way, trampled by horses, which made me wonder about something." I shook my head, already anticipating his reaction to my next question. "Daniel, what if their deaths weren't accidents?"

I couldn't see his face, but I could feel his eyes on me.

"You think Cora murdered them?"

"No, I'm just wondering, that's all. Emma said Cora hasn't been the same since the deaths, and it's easy to see how true that is. And there's that fear she has that her father will find out something. Yesterday, when she called me Em, she said she should've been braver, she should've never done what she did."

I turned to him, searching the dark for just one glimpse of his face. "Do you think there was bad blood between them all?"

"I don't know, Mercy."

"I wish I'd thought to ask Emma, but I guess it'll have to wait till Christmas Day now."

Clouds parted, and under the moon's bright face, I saw pure misery in Daniel's eyes. "Cora's father will be here by then," he whispered.

I nodded and shivered hard. Just hearing the words had set up an indescribable dread in me.

I WAS CAREFUL not to wear my hair like Emma's again. The next days passed quickly and without mishap, though the recently discovered jigsaw pieces of the past never stopped rattling around in my head. I explored the possibility of Mrs. Wilder being responsible for the loss of her mother and brother, but I couldn't bring myself to believe it of her. Their deaths had to be accidents, like everyone said.

Mrs. Wilder grew increasingly jittery as Christmas Eve approached, but trips to town seemed to lift her spirits. She'd creep into the house with her arms full of bundles and slip up the back stairs to hide away her purchases before Gabe and Gilly saw them.

Though still cold, Monday morning dawned clear and sunny, a perfect day for walking in the woods. Daniel had an early appointment with Dr. Kellam, but when he returned, he and I were to take the children to cut a Christmas tree. "A large one," Mrs. Wilder said, like her father had always insisted upon when she was small.

She packed a picnic lunch for us and said she'd have mugs of hot cider waiting when we got home. I wondered whether

Daniel could handle cutting down a tree with his leg the way it was, but he didn't seem worried.

While I waited for him to return, I sat with the children at the table, helping them make paper ornaments for the tree. Just last year I'd done the same with Mama and the kids, laughing about how, next Christmas, we'd have to hang all our ornaments halfway up the branches to keep Honor from pulling them down.

Honor. It hurt to think of her; I missed her little face so. I closed my eyes against the pain, wishing I could stop dwelling on what could never be. Yet it was impossible to keep my family out of my thoughts. Memories came at me from everywhere. Scattered across this very table, I imagined I saw Mama's paper angels, Justice's crooked stars, and Charity's snowflake garlands.

I reached for a stack of white paper, hoping I could remember how Charity had made her delicate garlands. I folded each piece with care, but when I began the intricate cuts, a sudden need to succeed trembled through my fingers and into the scissors. Somehow I *had* to make every cut right. It felt as though I'd lose her all over again if I didn't. I paused, willing away the anxious tremor, and began again.

When I finished, I set the scissors aside, and with breathless concentration I unfolded the paper and held it up. The kids cheered. It was a perfect copy of my sister's artistry. My heart cheered, too, reaching out to her, saying, Look, Charity! I finally did it. You were a better teacher than you ever knew.

Daniel burst through the door, smelling of crisp cold air, and walked crutch-free into the kitchen. He still had a slight limp, but it didn't seem to slow him down. The kids shouted and ran to him, chattering about all the things they could do together again. I bundled them up for the trip, and we all piled into Mrs. Wilder's shiny black Ford.

"How far is it to the trees?" Gabe asked as we bumped along.

"About five miles."

"Is that far?" Gilly wanted to know.

Daniel grinned at me. "It's about like walking into town three times from our house. Can you hold up three fingers, Gillykins?"

I laughed at the nickname, but she didn't bat an eye. She studied her fingers, found the right number, then held up her hand.

"Somebody is learning to count," he said.

She nodded. "Mercy teached me." She looked at her fingers again. "That's really, really far, Daniel," she said.

"Not too far for us," Gabe said, "'cause we got Daniel and Mama's Ford. We're gonna bring home a *big* tree."

Daniel couldn't stop grinning.

About ten minutes later, he pulled off the road and parked. He grabbed the picnic basket and ax, and we all headed into the woods.

It took far longer for the kids to choose a tree than for Daniel to cut it down. No sooner would they settle on one than they were running off again, shouting, "Wait, this one's better!" He didn't seem to mind, though. When the tree was finally chosen and cut, we spread a blanket on the ground and unpacked the sandwiches Mrs. Wilder had made for us. Gabe and Gilly ate theirs lying on their backs, staring at the clouds.

"I want to fly airplanes when I grow up," Gabe said.

"Well, I'm gonna be a bird when I grow up," Gilly told him.

"You can't be a bird, silly. You're already a girl." He turned to me, laughing. "That's crazy, isn't it, Mercy?"

I lay down beside him, gazing up at the clouds, remembering how I'd done the very same thing just this past spring with Charity and Justice. Longing for just one more glimpse of them, I reached for Gabe's hand and let myself go back to the field of wind-tossed black-eyed Susans and that wide blue sky, but only for the briefest of moments. Any longer and I'd dip too deep into that never-ending sea of grief inside me.

"Oh, I don't know, Gabe," I said, pushing my thoughts back to the present. "I remember when I wished I could be a bird, too. I used to lie on my back like this and look up at the clouds for so long, I felt just like I was flying."

"Really?" he asked.

"Sure. Give it a try."

The kids were quiet for a while. Then Gilly flapped her arms and yelled, "Look at me! I'm a bird!"

"That's nothing," Gabe said. "I'm an airplane, and I'm so high birds can't even see me!"

Daniel was grinning again, saying he wanted to fly, too. He

scooted next to me and put his head close to mine, but when I glanced his way, he wasn't looking at the sky. His green eyes were on me.

My head did a dizzy spin, and I jerked upright, embarrassed. "It's getting late," I said. "We should land and start packing up."

The kids complained, but they were soon chattering again about their flights. All the way home, Gabe asked questions like "How do airplanes fly if they don't flap their wings?" Gilly just wanted to know when she was going to grow feathers.

True to her word, Mrs. Wilder was waiting with cider when we got home, and we gathered around the fireplace with steaming mugs to tell her about our day.

"We got the best tree in the whole forest, Mama," Gabe said.

"Yeah, the best!" Gilly shouted. "And we went flying!"

"Flying?"

"Yeah," Gabe said. "I was an airplane, and Gilly was—"

"I was a bird, Mama! Way up in the clouds."

Mrs. Wilder gave us a puzzled glance, but Daniel just grinned and shrugged. He cranked up the Victrola and played "Shine On, Harvest Moon" and then "The Darktown Strutters' Ball." Gabe and Gilly danced, and for a while, Mrs. Wilder was full of smiles, happy to be watching the kids twirl around, and captivated by their adventures in the woods.

When the music ended, I saw the tender hugs she gave them and was finally convinced. There could never be enough hate in her actually to harm someone. Certainly not her own mother or brother. What was she so afraid of?

I GOT UP hours before daylight the next morning to start my holiday baking. I would be making bread and desserts, but first I'd work on my gift to the family. It wasn't much. Just big gingerbread stars with each person's name in icing. I planned to hang them on the tree tomorrow morning, before anyone woke up.

There'd be lots to do today. Mr. Collier would arrive by surrey around noon—a fact I thought strange in light of the way his wife and son had died, but Mrs. Wilder said her father had no patience with automobiles. She, on the other hand, would ride in nothing else. According to Daniel, she refused even to stand near a horse or wagon.

Mrs. Wilder had risen early that morning, too, but I'd known I couldn't count on her for much. She was far too fretful to do more than arrange garlands of greenery over the mantel and up the front staircase railing. I did my best to ease her worry, but nothing I said seemed to help for long.

By late morning, the house smelled of yeasty bread, sage, and cinnamon. Hens sat waiting in the icebox, cleaned and ready for stuffing, and apple cake, pumpkin pies, and loaves of braided bread cooled on the table. The gingerbread cookies were hidden away in my room.

I'd taken care of Mr. Collier's bedding the day before. It smelled sweet and fresh, and I made sure that every surface in his room had been oiled and polished.

Everything was almost ready. While I set the table for the simple noon meal that Mrs. Wilder requested, Daniel brought in the tree. I heard the kids chattering about where it should go, and when I peeked into the parlor, the big tree sat near the windows, filling the whole corner.

"Now, get up to your room," Daniel told them, "and change into the clothes Mercy pressed for you. Your grandfather will be here any minute."

They thundered up the stairs but came back down shortly, asking me for help with buttons and ribbons.

"There, now," I told them when I'd finished. "You look wonderful. Your grandfather will be very proud of you."

They scrambled to the parlor windows to watch for Mr. Collier's arrival, and none too soon.

"Someone's coming!" Gabe yelled right away. He pointed to the road. "It's Grandfather!"

We hurried outside to see two shiny black horses pull a large, sleek surrey up to the house. Gabe and Gilly rushed down the steps with Daniel close behind, but Mrs. Wilder watched from the porch, her face ashen and lifeless. I stood beside her, powerless to ease her distress.

The tall, well-dressed man smiled at the kids through a gray handlebar mustache and shook Gabe's hand, making his gold watch fob bounce and sparkle in the midday sun. While Daniel took the reins and led the horses toward the barn, Mr. Collier gave his coat a quick brush and strode toward the porch to embrace his daughter.

She glanced at me, eyes wide with dread, and for a moment I thought she might faint. But, like a limp marionette whose invisible strings were suddenly wrenched tight, she straightened her back and lifted her chin. Mr. Collier hugged her briefly, expressing his sorrow at her loss, then pulled away, revealing a staggering darkness in his daughter's face. I shot him a startled glance, but he'd already turned toward the door. He hadn't seen.

I began to breathe easier, but I knew my relief would only be temporary. From what I knew of Mrs. Wilder, she'd never be able to hide her feelings, and if it happened again, there'd be no explaining away what I'd seen mirrored in her eyes.

Mrs. Wilder hated her father.

"The bravest thing you can do when you are not brave
is to profess courage and act accordingly."

CORRA MAY WHITE HARRIS

chapter
26

WITH JUST THAT one murderous look, everything I'd ever questioned about Mrs. Wilder came rushing back to me. Regardless
of what I wanted to believe, I couldn't be sure what this woman
might be capable of.

I left Mr. Collier in the parlor to talk to his excited grand-
children and pulled his daughter into the kitchen, pretending
to need help with the noon meal. I didn't dare leave her alone
with them. It would be terrible if the children witnessed what
I'd just seen in their mother's face.

I picked up the tray of egg-salad sandwiches I'd made
earlier. "Would you mind very much finishing up the tea, Mrs.
Wilder?" I asked.

She looked at me, her eyes still dark and unpredictable, and
with a nod, she went to the sink.

My fingers trembled around the tray. I glanced out the
kitchen window. What could be taking Daniel so long? I set
the sandwiches on the dining-room table and returned to
slice apples and cheese.

A second glance toward the barn showed Daniel making
his way back to the house. While Mrs. Wilder took the tea into

the dining room, he slipped through the kitchen door, took one look at my face, and asked, "What's wrong?"

"We'll have to talk later," I whispered. "But watch her, Daniel. Please, don't leave her alone with her father."

Mrs. Wilder came back into the kitchen with an empty tray, and I returned to my plate of apples and cheese before Daniel could say another word.

When everything was ready, Mr. Collier seated himself at the head of the table. I saw Gabe flinch, then give his grandfather a hard look. The man was sitting in his father's place. Daniel whispered something in Gabe's ear that seemed to help, and though the boy still looked disgruntled, he leaned back.

The light meal progressed with questions from Mr. Collier about Daniel's plans for his future and the parcel of land his father had left him. Daniel said little, only that he expected to help his stepmother raise his brother and sister.

I sat back, quietly observing, and Mr. Collier didn't seem the least bit bothered by my silence. After all, I was just hired help, someone who should be taking meals in the kitchen, not sitting at the dining table like family.

Mrs. Wilder continued to glare at her father, a detail that surely hadn't escaped him. He found her easy enough to ignore, however, choosing instead to chat with Gabe about fishing and to tease Gilly into rolling giggles. I was grateful the kids were too busy to notice their mother.

After a while, I relaxed somewhat, a fact that surprised me.

I supposed it was because the man had a contagious laugh and an easy charm about him. I even found myself wondering what it was that Mrs. Wilder despised so much. Daniel appeared calmer, too, caught up in the tide of Mr. Collier's remarkable ability to beguile.

When the meal was over, Mr. Collier went to his room to rest. I sent the kids up, too, reassuring them that after they napped they could trim the tree. I knew the next few hours of waiting would be difficult for them, though. They were far too excited to sleep.

Mrs. Wilder helped a bit with the dishes, then went up as well. As soon as she was gone, Daniel found me in the kitchen.

"What happened?" he whispered, keeping an eye on the back stairs. "Why were you so worried about Cora being alone with her father?"

I hesitated, remembering Mr. Collier's charm, wondering if I'd made a mistake. But no. Mrs. Wilder's eyes had sent a clear message.

"Did you see her?" I asked. "Did you see the way she looked at her father?"

He nodded. "I've seen that expression before, once during his last visit, and again not very long ago." He looked away, focusing on another time. "I promised Father I'd never speak of it, but he would expect me to put the kids first. He'd agree that I can't keep covering for her."

"Covering for what?"

"Well, it wasn't really her fault, Mercy. She's sick, and I found that out only too well the day she knocked me down the stairs."

"*She* broke your leg?"

He shrugged. "Like I said, she didn't mean to. It was because of what she saw in my hand."

"But, Daniel, whatever could make her do such a horrible thing?"

He shrugged again, as if he could hardly believe it himself. "A yellow pencil."

I tossed him a skeptical look.

"The day it happened, Father had finally decided to tutor the kids himself. He asked me to tell Cora to buy more pencils the next time she was in Hilliard's store. I picked one up and ran into Cora just outside the door on the staircase landing. When she saw the pencil, her face turned a deadly white and she shoved past me. I lost my footing. I remember hearing her bedroom door slam shut as I tumbled down the stairs."

"I just don't understand." I stared at him, trying to make some sense out of what he was saying.

"At the time, I didn't, either. Days later, Father told me why she'd been so frightened. As children, she and Devon had been strapped severely for answering school questions incorrectly, even locked in a dark closet at times. I guess yellow pencils remind her of that."

I couldn't speak. I kept thinking of all the broken pencils I'd seen on the porch my first time here. How could the man we saw today be brutal enough to whip his own children over a wrong answer? And if he did, could that kind of cruelty breed a murderous heart? I thought of Gabe and Gilly, and fear rumbled through me.

"Oh, Daniel," I whispered, "we can't leave the two of them alone for even a minute. The children . . ."

He flinched. "I know, I know."

"Maybe I shouldn't leave tomorrow."

He shook his head. "It's best if you go on to the Glory, Mercy. Tell Mrs. Sayers that Cora is worse. She knows her best. Maybe she can help us."

His face darkened with such fearful worry that all I wanted was to make it go away, erase it like scribbles on a chalkboard, and see him smile again, the way he did yesterday, tromping through the woods with the kids. Yet I was as frightened as he was.

"We'll manage till tomorrow," Daniel said.

I nodded. "And Emma will help; I know she will."

He moved closer and reached for me. "I hope so," he whispered.

I let him wrap his arms around me while all the promises I'd made to myself reared up, urging me to push him away. But he was alone and worried about his family. He needed this small comfort.

chapter 27

DANIEL FETCHED his stepmother's special box of ornaments from the attic, the ones her mother had treasured before her death, and set them on the parlor table. Mrs. Wilder opened the lid slowly, and when she touched the colorful decorations, I saw her slip away, escaping to that safe place she'd find when her world became too difficult. I'd seen it happen before, seen the glazed look in her eyes, the one she had now as she smiled at the kids and hung a painted angel on the tree. She had to be missing her husband terribly at a time like this. I missed my family, too, and understood how bleak the loss could be. But at least she'd found a peace of sorts, even if it was only a temporary one.

I went back to the kitchen to work, but instead of hens and stuffing, I saw Mama spread a blanket on the ground, saying we *must* see the sky exactly the way the three wise men must have seen it. I heard Papa's deep voice telling the story of Baby Jesus, and I remembered how it came to life against the vast starry sky. We sang carols, too, while Papa played his harmonica, but no one sang "Silent Night" the way Mama did. I closed my eyes and I could still hear it, *feel* it, sweet and pure, filling me up, beautiful enough to make a grown man cry. And my papa often did.

Laughter from the parlor pulled me back to my work. Gabe and Gilly were obviously keeping everyone busy trimming the tree, and soon I even heard Christmas carols coming from the Victrola. I smiled, glad that Daniel would have no time for pondering darker matters. He appeared caught up in the magic of Christmas as thoroughly as any child.

It was hard not to think of home again while I filled Mrs. Wilder's crystal water goblets and put platters of stuffed hen and acorn squash on the table. I'd never had a Christmas Eve supper as grand as this, nor had I ever dreamed I would, though I'd read about them many times in Papa's books. It was peculiar to find myself here in this house with this family, as if I'd been caught up in a powerful wind, shaken fiercely from top to bottom, and dropped into the pages of Charity's *Jane Eyre*. I scarcely recognized myself anymore. Even as I faced one change, another cropped up, and before I knew it, God had turned another page.

Was it only weeks ago that I'd been with Miz Beulah, dreaming of home? Back then I had every reason to believe I'd be sitting with Mama and the kids at the Bonners' table this very night. I closed my eyes, picturing us there, laughter ringing, the magic of Christmas alive in every eye; then I let the dream fade away. I felt the ache, the sick longing, the pure misery of my loss creeping up inside me once more, and choked back tears.

Mama, Papa, and the kids were gone, and that was a fact I had to accept. I was here, now, with *this* family, tangled up in the Wilders' fifteen-year-old secrets. The mystery of how I'd so quickly come to this odd place in my life was never far from my thoughts, and I couldn't help wondering what else I'd find when God turned yet another page in my book.

Write it yourself, Mercy.

My head jerked up from my work.

"Mama?" I whispered.

The kitchen was empty, just as I knew it was, and yet my heart drummed and my hands shook as if I expected at any moment to see Mama standing right in front of me. Her voice had been that clear. But it wasn't hearing her voice that made me most uneasy. It was the words. Write it myself? She'd never said anything like that to me before.

I peered around the room, wondering again if it had all been in my head or if she could've possibly . . .

Oh, but it would *have* to wait. Supper was ready.

I uncorked the wine Mr. Collier had brought with him, set it near his plate, and went to the parlor.

"Look, Mercy!" Gilly shouted, pointing to the tree.

"We used your snowflakes," Gabe said.

They grabbed my hands and pulled me to the tree to see the white garlands draped limb to limb.

"It's beautiful," I whispered, thinking of how pleased Charity would've been. "This must be the most handsome tree in all of Canton."

"It is! It is!" they shouted.

I turned to their mother, who'd been sitting quietly in her chair. "Supper is ready, Mrs. Wilder, whenever you are."

She looked up at me with that vacant stare of hers, then blinked it away. "Thank you, Mercy. It smells wonderful." She rose from her seat. "Shall we all go in?"

Daniel and I rounded up the kids behind their mother and herded them into the dining room. Mr. Collier followed and took his seat at the head of the table again. I glanced at Gabe. Whatever Daniel had said earlier had softened the boy's anger to only an occasional frustrated glance.

After the blessing, Mr. Collier poured his wine and drank heartily before beginning his meal. As he ate, he refilled his glass often and talked increasingly about the house and the eighty acres bequeathed to his daughter.

Mrs. Wilder didn't seem to mind. She'd retreated to her safe place again and sat without comment throughout the meal. It soon became clear, however, that Daniel had no such place to go. The muscles in his face tensed and strained. The more Mr. Collier talked of possibilities for the eighty-acre parcel, the more fire I saw in Daniel's eyes. I was coming to suspect, as Daniel must have, that Mr. Collier had plans of his own for this land.

I was grateful to see the meal end, and even more so to see Mr. Collier retire to his room. Mrs. Wilder kissed the kids good night, wished them sweet dreams, then leaned close, her eyes more alive than I'd seen them all day.

"After you put the children to bed," she whispered, "would you help me carry down their presents?"

I smiled and nodded, excited at such pleasurable work. I mentioned it to Daniel while I cleaned the kitchen, and he was quick to tell me not to worry, that he'd stay with the kids till they were sound asleep.

When the dishes were washed, we went up together to tuck the kids into bed.

"I wanna hear the story about Baby Jesus and the star," Gabe said.

Gilly threw back her quilts and scrambled out of bed. "Me, too! I'll get it."

Daniel picked her up and tucked her back in bed. "You'd best cover up again or your toes will freeze. *I'll* get it."

He reached for their Bible stories, and I waved good night to them all, leaving Daniel to read the story of Christmas.

I knocked lightly on Mrs. Wilder's door, and we began the careful trek up and down the stairs, carrying packages tied in colorful ribbon to put under the tree. I'd already decided to stay away from the parlor tomorrow morning. It would be far too strange to take part in another family's gift-giving, but in addition to that, I feared it would make me feel even more alone. I was grateful to have so much to do in the kitchen. Besides, I wanted this Christmas meal to be the best ever.

When we were done, I stood with Mrs. Wilder in the soft lamplight, appraising a scene that looked as if it had come straight from a fairy tale.

She put her arm around me and gave my shoulder a warm squeeze. "It's really beautiful, isn't it?"

I nodded, my throat too tight to answer.

"My prayers tonight will be for you and your sweet family, Mercy, but especially for both our mothers, for we know how much they loved their children, don't we?"

I could do nothing but stare at her. It seemed such an odd thing to hear in light of the questionable way her mother had died. I grappled for an explanation, some self-serving reason for her comment about mothers, but all I could see was love in her eyes.

"You'll pray for my darling Samuel, too, won't you?" she asked.

I could barely speak. "Yes, of course," I whispered, wiping at the sudden wetness on my cheeks.

"They're with us now, you know." The corners of her mouth lifted in a wistful smile. "When you're quiet, you can feel them."

I WENT TO my room in a daze, wondering about Mrs. Wilder's relationship with her mother. The kind and caring woman I'd seen tonight couldn't have killed her mother. In fact, if I were to trust all the heart signs I'd gotten from Mrs. Wilder, I would've said she wasn't capable of harming anyone.

I shed my dress and pulled my nightgown over my head, more confused than ever.

"They're with us," she'd said, which made me wonder about what I'd heard in the kitchen tonight.

Not once had I really believed the voice in my head was Mama's. I figured it was just me, remembering things she would've said if she were here. But this time felt different. She'd never said anything like *that* before. "Write it yourself"? I didn't even know what that meant.

I glanced out the window. The moon hadn't risen yet, but a blanket of stars lit the clear black heavens as brightly as jewels in a king's crown. I crawled into bed, pulled the covers up to my chin, and lay very still.

"When you're quiet, you can feel them," she'd said.

I WOKE DURING the night to more voices, but this time Mama's wasn't one of them. These were angry sounds, or at least one of them was. The muffled words twisted inside me and prickled up my spine. I threw on my robe, but even before I reached the door, the ominous mutterings had faded.

Upstairs, the hall was quiet, and no lights shone beneath bedroom doors. I peeked inside the kids' room. They were fast asleep. Had Daniel slept through it, too?

I stood in the dark, wondering if I'd dreamed it, but I knew in my heart I hadn't. I'd definitely heard Mr. Collier's deep voice, and the other had to be that of his daughter. My thoughts rambled through all that might've brought on an argument between them, but there really wasn't much a hired girl could do. Obviously they'd given up and retreated to their rooms, and I had no choice but to return to mine as well. I'd keep the door open a crack, though, just in case it happened again.

I crawled back into bed, knowing full well that I wouldn't sleep. The knot of secrets in this house seemed to be unraveling. Whatever had lain buried between Mrs. Wilder and her father for all those years might finally see daylight.

And tomorrow, for sure, the sun would rise on us all.

chapter
28

THOUGH I DIDN'T think it possible, I slept. Yet, long before daylight on this blessed Christmas morning, I was awake again,
fearful that something bad might've happened while I dozed. I
tiptoed up the stairs, only to find that all was quiet.

Relieved, I went back to my room, dressed, and pulled out
the gingerbread stars I'd made for the family. I hung them on
the tree with red ribbon, a big star for each of the Wilders—
Mr. Collier, too—with their names written in white icing. I
remembered how excited I'd been when Mama did the same for
us one Christmas. There hadn't been enough money for gifts
that year, but we'd gotten those magical stars.

I stood back, pleased. The five giant cookies looked beautiful. I knew they'd be enjoyed, but with so many wonderful gifts
beneath the tree, I also knew they'd never bring the same kind
of delight to this family that I'd experienced on that Christmas
morning long ago.

Just thinking of Mama, Papa, and the kids again had
brought on another sick pang of loss. It caught me unprepared,
as it often did, and I leaned hard against Mrs. Wilder's chair,

limp and trembling, willing the now familiar ache to pass. I was learning that distraction worked best. After a few moments, I gladly forced my attention to the fireplace. When I had a fire crackling, I went back to the kitchen to light the stove. I wanted to have fresh cinnamon rolls rising before anyone came down.

I was slicing the rolls when I heard the first stirrings. I put down my knife and listened.

Loud whispers, then footsteps in the hallway upstairs.

Excited giggles.

Light rapping, followed by laughter—Mrs. Wilder's.

"Yes, yes, I'm awake!" I heard her say. "Now go wake up Daniel while I get dressed."

More giggles. More footsteps drumming hard against the floor overhead.

A loud pounding.

"Daniel!" Gilly's voice. "Mama said get up!"

"It's Christmas!" Gabe yelled.

I spread a clean cup towel over the pan of cinnamon rolls, left them to rise by the stove, and hurried to watch for the kids.

When they saw me they shouted, "Merry Christmas!" and thundered down the stairs. After a quick hug, they pulled me into the parlor to see the tree. I listened for a moment to their excitement upon finding the stars, then slipped away.

I wanted to watch it all, but I'd made my decision last night not to interfere. Mr. Collier wouldn't like it, I was sure. Besides, there was breakfast to finish and still so much to do before the big noon meal would be ready. Mrs. Wilder had given me her recipe for a casserole I'd never made before, a dish prepared with last summer's canned corn and tomatoes, and I was nervous about it turning out just the way she liked.

I was making icing for the cinnamon rolls when Daniel stuck his head in the doorway, grinning. He held up his star.

"Did Santa Claus bring these?" he asked.

I smiled. "I never give away Santa's secrets."

"Then you must help me find a way to thank him later, okay?"

I laughed, pleased, and slid the rolls into the oven. While they baked, I fried sausage and potatoes, and when it was all ready, I went to the parlor to fetch the family.

Mrs. Wilder, surrounded by piles of wrapping paper, saw me before I could announce that breakfast was ready. She held her gingerbread star in her hand.

"Dear Mercy," she said, smiling up at me, "please come join us."

Uneasy, I stole a quick glance at her father, then shook my head. "Thank you, Mrs. Wilder, but breakfast is ready, and I should get back to the kitchen. I'll be making that tomato-corn casserole soon, and I want it to turn out just the way you remember it."

"Ha!" Mr. Collier bellowed, poking Gabe in the belly with a long, wide finger. "I smell cinnamon rolls, and I'm gonna make sure I get my share."

Gabe laughed. "Me, too, Grandfather!"

I chose not to join them around the table, but I should've known that Daniel would come to check on me. He looked around the busy kitchen and nodded. "I was afraid this might be too much for you. Come eat with us, and then I'll help."

I shook my head. "I just wanted to get everything done early. As soon as the meal is ready for the oven, I'll leave Mrs. Wilder to finish up, and go on to the Glory. Did you hear the voices last night?" I whispered.

He gave me a puzzled look. "I didn't hear anything."

"Someone was arguing, and if you weren't a part of it, then it had to be Mrs. Wilder and her father."

"What did you hear?"

"Nothing I could make out, but they sounded angry. By the time I got upstairs, it was over."

He nodded. "They haven't said a word to each other all morning."

I pitched a nervous glance toward the dining room. "You'd better get back in there."

"Okay, but I'll be back soon to help."

I nodded my thanks and pushed him toward the door.

DANIEL REPORTED LATER that, though breakfast had been cordial, something unspoken had definitely bristled between Mr. Collier and his daughter. He was worried, and I was, too, especially when I overheard Mr. Collier ask Daniel to ready the surrey.

"You're not leaving us already, are you?" Daniel asked.

"No, not at all," he said. "I thought I'd take Cora out later. It's a beautiful day, and a little fresh air would do her good."

I put down my mixing spoon, walked to the doorway, and peered at Mrs. Wilder. She sat motionless, staring at her father with that same staggering darkness I'd seen before. A ride in a horse-drawn surrey couldn't be something she wanted. Surely she'd refuse.

I saw Daniel toss an inquiring glance at his stepmother, and when she didn't respond, he turned back to Mr. Collier with a nod. "Yessir. I'll take care of it."

I returned to the kitchen, confused, wishing I could talk to Mrs. Wilder, make sure she was okay. What did her father hope to accomplish on a drive like that? She hated horses and wagons, didn't she?

I hurried through the rest of the preparations, and finally called Mrs. Wilder into the kitchen.

"Everything's almost ready," I told her. "All you have to do is check on the ham now and then." I pointed to the stove. "The fruit glaze is in the pan, and everything else is on the worktable, covered and waiting."

"Thank you, Mercy. I don't know what I would've done without your help." She gave me a hug and untied my apron. "Now you go see your friends and have a lovely day."

I nodded, but I couldn't bring myself to leave yet.

"Um . . . Mrs. Wilder?"

She turned back to me, and I fidgeted, knowing full well this was no business of mine and she could easily tell me so.

"About the drive with your father, are you sure you want to go? I mean, surely Mr. Collier would understand—"

"Don't *worry*." She patted my hand. "Things have a way of working out just the way they're supposed to."

MRS. WILDER HAD given me such a confident smile, all I could do was nod and fetch my coat, but something about her assurance troubled me till the moment Emma pulled me into her kitchen with a boisterous "Merry Christmas."

"Where's Beth?" I asked.

"Upstairs with Vera. They're gonna walk over to the Wilders'." She pointed to a small package sitting on the table. "Vera has a gift for the kids."

"That was sweet of her."

"Nice for us, too. I got stuffed ducks in the oven, a big pan of those greens you like, and berry cobbler with sweet cream. It's all done. We got nothin' to do but talk while the girls are gone." She poured us a cup of her special spiced tea. "Now tell me 'bout Christmas at the Wilders'."

Her request churned up all the uneasiness I'd been living with, and the moment I looked up at her, I could tell she knew.

"Mr. Collier?" she asked.

I nodded.

"Figures."

I didn't have a chance to say more. I heard voices on the

landing upstairs and waited while Vera and Beth made their way down. They looked up at me, surprised.

"I didn't hear you come in," Beth said, grinning. "Merry Christmas, Mercy."

"And to you, too," I said.

Vera waved. "Nice to see you again."

"Thank you, Vera. Emma tells me you're planning to do some Christmas visiting."

She nodded. "We won't be long, though. Papa wouldn't like it if I missed dinner." She picked up the package and headed for the door.

"See you soon," Beth said.

Emma waved goodbye, watched the girls leave, then turned to me, her smile gone. "Is Cora okay?"

"Yes. I mean, I don't know. Maybe. For now anyway."

"You don't sound too sure of yourself."

I shook my head. "I'm sorry, Emma. I guess I'm just confused about all that's been happening. The only thing I know for sure is that Mrs. Wilder isn't handling her father's visit very well."

"That ain't so surprisin', Mercy."

"I know, but Daniel and I are worried. Yesterday I saw something in her eyes I'd never seen before."

"What was that?"

"Oh, Emma," I moaned. "Surely you know the woman hates her father."

"Well, that ain't a surprisin' fact, either, you know?"

"What do you mean?"

Emma took a long sip of her tea. "Maybe you just oughta tell me what else you're confused about."

I blew out a frustrated breath. "Okay. Last night I heard arguing between Mrs. Wilder and her father. I couldn't tell what they were saying, but he sounded quite angry. By the time I got upstairs, it was over. They'd gone back to their rooms."

She gave me a thoughtful look and set her cup down. "Look, none of what you're sayin' is that outlandish. I ain't never expected more from either of 'em. The old man is a mean, selfish jackass who ain't got an ounce of patience for the word 'no,' and Cora always did hate any kind of fracas. She took the easy road ever' chance she got."

I nodded slowly. This wasn't going well, and I dreaded the thought of telling Daniel about how badly I'd done. I rummaged through more memories of the last few days. "Did you know about the pencils?"

She gave me a baffled look.

"Mr. Collier used to beat her, Emma—Devon, too—and lock them in closets every time they got their lessons wrong."

"Oh, that. Yeah, I knew. Everybody in that house knew. I told you the old man was a jackass, but no one was brave enough to stand up against him."

"Okay, then, tell me how Mrs. Wilder feels about horses."

Emma raised an eyebrow and looked up at me. "She don't like 'em much."

"Would it be like her to accept a drive in a surrey?"

"Nope, wouldn't be like her at all."

"Well, she did, Emma. Mr. Collier insisted, and she didn't complain."

A frown tugged at Emma's forehead. "Why do you think he wanted to take her on a drive?"

I shrugged. "Might have something to do with the land. Mr. Collier talked a lot last night about the eighty acres Mr. Wilder left her. Daniel thinks he wants it."

"The land," Emma whispered. She stared out the window. "And you say Cora agreed to go on this drive?"

I nodded. "When I asked about it, she told me not to worry, that . . . let's see. She said, 'Things have a way of working out just the way they're supposed to.'"

Something odd swept over Emma's face. She blinked a few times, like she'd been sitting in a dark room and someone had just yanked back the curtains. She shoved her cup aside, grabbed my coat, and jerked the door open.

"Mercy, get back to the Wilders', and whatever you do, don't let Cora leave with her father. Don't even let her near that surrey, you hear? I'll come by quick as I can and have a good talk with her."

I stumbled down the steps, full of questions, but one look at Emma's face told me I'd better not take time to ask a thing. I took off running and didn't stop till I reached the Wilders' front porch.

I burst through the door, looking for Daniel, but no one was there except Beth.

"Where's Daniel?" I gasped, trying to catch my breath.

"He's upstairs with Vera and the kids," she said.

"And Mrs. Wilder?"

"She's on a drive with her father."

I cringed and glanced up at her, still panting so hard I could hardly speak. "Get Daniel . . . and tell Vera . . . to stay with the kids."

Beth just stood there, looking confused.

"Now!"

She hurried up the stairs, calling for Daniel. He met her at the top of the landing, then ran to me, eyes wide. "What's wrong?"

"We have to find them." I sucked in a deep breath. "Emma said not to let them out of our sight."

"I know where they went," he said. "Come on."

We ran to Mrs. Wilder's Ford. Daniel cranked the starter and jumped in, and we took off across the pasture, bumping toward the creek. I hung on, praying that whatever had gotten Emma so stirred up wasn't happening.

It seemed the ride would take forever, but before too long we caught sight of the horses. The surrey stood empty, near the creek where Daniel thought it would be. He slowed and stopped.

"What now?" I asked.

"We walk," he said. "But quietly. Might be better if they don't know we're here."

I nodded and got out.

A dry north wind ruffled the winter grasses, sending brown

waves ahead of us, rushing toward the creek. I followed them, hardly aware of the chill.

To avoid startling the horses, we changed our approach and stole around to the side. Mrs. Wilder and her father stood in a clearing near the surrey, not far from the creek. Like last night, I heard only muffled voices at first, but they quickly turned into discernible words. At a safe distance, Daniel pulled me behind a large cedar tree to watch and listen.

"You and the children can live with *me*, you know," Mr. Collier was saying. "You can manage the house for me."

Mrs. Wilder gave him a squint-eyed look. "You think you can steal everything my husband worked so hard for and turn me into a maid?" She shook her head. "Believe me, I'm not going to stand by and watch you do to my children what you did to your own."

"Don't be a ninny, Cora. You can't work this land. It would only be a burden to you."

"It will belong to Gabriel and Gillian one day. They'll work it. They'll make it worth something."

Mr. Collier's face showed flagrant disgust. "You sound like your mother."

"Ah," she said, nodding. "So I do. You did the same thing to her, didn't you?"

"You don't know what you're talking about," he said with a sneer.

"But I do, Father." She slid a hand into her skirt pocket. "Mother wanted Devon and me to have Grandfather's farm, but you sold it for yourself."

She'd said the words with confidence, and Mr. Collier's smugness wavered.

"I was there. I saw you arguing." She pulled the big black button out of her pocket and held it up. "It's from your coat, remember? Mother died with it in her hand. You can't have forgotten how she died, now, can you, Father?"

A sudden glimmer of satisfaction danced in her eyes, and Mr. Collier's face turned deep red. "This is lunacy!" he bellowed. "You weren't even there."

"I saw you hit her. Over and over again." She shot him a lethal look. "You killed her, then you got scared and ran the wagon over her so it would look like an accident. You did the same to poor Devon, too, when you found out he'd married Emma, didn't you?"

Daniel gave me a startled glance, and when we looked again, we saw Mr. Collier's eyes narrow and his lip curl. "Why, you little . . ."

He took a step toward his daughter, fists clenched, but when she didn't flinch, he hesitated.

"I'm not the coward I used to be," she said coolly. "I won't run away and hide this time." She reached in her bag and pulled out a revolver. "My biggest regret is that I didn't tell anyone what you did in time to save Devon."

I coiled, ready to run to her, but Daniel grabbed me and held me back. He gave his head a determined shake.

"Where'd you get that?" Mr. Collier asked, pointing at the gun.

"Samuel bought it for me years ago."

"You don't know anything about guns. You never shot a Colt in your life."

"You've been gone a long time, Father. If you walk out to the garden shed you'll find the targets Samuel set up for me." She gave him a sly smile. "I'm an excellent shot."

Mr. Collier's expression shifted to one of doubt. He circled slowly toward the other side of the clearing, forcing Mrs. Wilder closer to the horses; then he let out a nervous laugh.

"If this is about the land, Cora, then keep it. It means nothing to me."

"Of course I'll keep it," she said with exaggerated assurance. "But this isn't about the land." She waved the gun at him. "It's about lies, Father. Fifteen years of lies. It's about Mother and Devon. It's about murder."

He muttered obscenities under his breath, then shouted, "Okay!" He swung his arms wide in a livid surrender. "What do you want from me?"

Mrs. Wilder smiled and whispered, "Nothing at all, Father. Not anymore."

She'd barely spoken loud enough for me to hear, but something in her voice made my skin prickle with alarm. I glanced at Mr. Collier. Despite the chill, sweat peppered his brow, and pure rage twisted his face. Clearly she'd pushed him too far, but it didn't seem to worry her.

She just raised the gun and aimed.

chapter
30

MY HEART BANGED so hard in my chest I feared it might be heard. Daniel's hand tightened around mine and pulled. We hurried toward Mrs. Wilder, but before we could reach her, a low growl rumbled from Mr. Collier. A second later, the man lunged, teeth bared, at his daughter.

He grabbed her gun arm with one hand and slammed his fist into her face with the other. She let out a piercing cry, startling the horses into a skittering dance, but she wouldn't let go of the gun.

They struggled, and a shot exploded, echoing all around us. The panicked horses reared. Mr. Collier flung his daughter to the ground, then turned, gun in hand, only to see hooves above his head.

Daniel leaped toward the surrey and worked frantically to grab the loose reins. I jerked Mrs. Wilder out of the way, flinching from the raining blows that fell so close to us, but I had no time to help her father. The frightened horses reared again and again, pummeling him into the ground.

Daniel finally calmed the horses, and when the dust settled, I saw him kneeling beside the crumpled man.

I looked down at Mrs. Wilder. Blood oozed from a dark hole in her chest, but she was still breathing.

"Daniel!" I hollered. "You have to get Doc Kellam!"

I pulled the bottom of her dress up, pressed it to the wound, and saw Daniel hurrying toward us.

"Mr. Collier—is he dead?" I asked.

Daniel nodded, yanked off his coat, and dropped to his knees to cover his stepmother.

"Can you hear me, Cora?" he asked.

Her eyes flickered open for a moment, then closed again.

"I'm leaving you with Mercy while I get the doctor." He kissed her forehead. "You'll be okay, you hear?" He ran for the Ford, yelling over his shoulder, "You'll be okay!"

THE NORTH WIND whispered through the clearing, rustling dead leaves and fingering through Mrs. Wilder's hair. I waited, only faintly aware that an eerie but blessed calm had come over me.

Her dress soaked up blood till it could hold no more. I pulled off my skirt and knelt in my petticoat to hold it tight against her wound, but the red stain still spread, creeping under my fingers, dripping, seeping into the ground. I didn't know a body could bleed so much.

Minutes crawled by. I leaned my forehead against Mrs. Wilder's and prayed she'd be okay.

"Her children need her," I whispered to God. "They've already lost a father."

Tears dripped off my nose, and I sat up to wipe them from Mrs. Wilder's cold cheek.

"There's been too much death," I scolded. "Too much! How many souls do You need?"

Seemingly in answer, warm sunlight crept across Mrs. Wilder's pale face, and soon even the chill wind died. I tossed a skeptical glance toward the heavens, then heard the chug of an engine. The sputtering sound shattered the curious calm that had enveloped me after Daniel left. I stared anew at the horror, and a sick panic gripped me. Oh, why didn't they hurry?

The Ford rolled to a stop just yards away, and Daniel, Doc Kellam, and Emma rushed toward me.

"I did everything I could think of," I told the doctor.

He tried to move me aside, but I couldn't let go.

"It's okay, Mercy," Doc Kellam said softly. "You can stop now." He gave my arm a gentle tug. "Don't worry; you did everything right."

I finally let him pull my hands from her wound, and sat back, fearful of what my heart already knew, afraid that Mrs. Wilder's life had already drained through my fingers.

Daniel pulled a handkerchief from his pocket and knelt close to me. He wiped my wet face and cleaned my bloody hands. I felt Emma beside me, too, and reached out to her, full of remorse.

"I'm so sorry, Emma. I was too late. She'd already left in the surrey with her father." I covered my face with my hands, heartsick at my failure.

Emma wrapped trembling arms around me and pulled me up. "Oh, honey," she moaned, her voice breaking with regret, "I'm the one who shoulda done more, not you."

I saw Daniel aim a questioning glance at the doctor, and Doc Kellam shook his head.

"She's gone," he said.

My knees shook and folded under me. I slid back to the ground beside Mrs. Wilder. Why did this keep happening to so many good people?

I tried, but this time I couldn't stop the tears. They poured from some flooded place inside me, a place so full of stormy loss I couldn't hold them back anymore.

Where are You, God? I wanted to shout. But He had already turned the page and moved on.

"DON'T WORRY," Emma said to Daniel. "Me and Doc Kellam will take care of everything, and I'll bring Cora's Ford back to you tomorrow. You two take the surrey and go on back home. You need to be with those children."

My mind jolted back to the kids. I glanced at Daniel and saw his eyes cloud with dread.

"How can I tell them?" he asked. His words cracked, shattering against the wretched task he faced.

"Mercy will help you," she said. "Together you'll find a way."

He gave Emma a slight nod, then helped load the lifeless bodies into the Ford. It wasn't till Daniel and I were on our way back to the house, however, that I realized just how far-reaching these deaths might be. Daniel and the kids would be changed forever, but my life would be altered again, too. Mrs. Wilder was gone, and it was a fact that the whole world frowned mightily upon a young hired girl living alone with a man. A cold dread shivered through me. I could never live in that house with Daniel now.

I looked ahead to what was coming, and from where I sat, the inescapable truth looked as black and stifling as death itself.

Mr. Collier had taken more than his daughter's life today. He'd taken another family from me.

We pulled up to the house, and Daniel tied the horses to the porch railing. "I'll bed them down later," he said, and held out his hand.

I could hardly get my body to move. I let him help me out of the surrey, leaning heavily on him, and together we walked across the porch, he without his blood-soaked coat and I without my skirt.

Beth swung the door wide and stood there gaping at the red smears on my petticoat.

"What *happened*?" she asked, straining to see the empty surrey behind us.

Daniel ignored her question. "Where are the kids?"

"Upstairs with Vera. Shall I get them?"

Daniel nodded. "Please."

She disappeared, and we sat on the parlor love seat to wait. I folded my petticoat to hide the red stains, then wrapped my arms around my belly, painfully aware that, in the midst of all this misery, the wounds from my own loss were bleeding again. That was bad enough, but I could hardly bear the thought of Gabe and Gilly suffering the same devastating anguish. It wasn't fair. They were too young. I felt a movement close by, and when I looked up, they were there, standing in front of us.

"We've been playing with Vera," Gabe said.

"Yeah," Gilly added, her face still bright with Christmas. "Santa brought me a new dolly, 'member? Wanna play, too?"

"Maybe later," Daniel said. He shot me a nervous glance. "We need to talk to you about something first."

Gilly pointed to my petticoat and giggled. "You look funny, Mercy."

Gabe had a more serious look on his face. Something wasn't right, and he knew it. "Where's Mama?" he wanted to know.

Daniel moved over and patted the seat between us. "Come sit with us, and I'll tell you," he said.

They scrambled onto the seat and gazed up at him expectantly, but something sick and dark had crept into Daniel's eyes. It pulled me up and around the love seat, where I stood beside him, my hand on his shoulder, trying to give him whatever strength was left inside me.

"Where's Mama?" Gabe asked again.

Daniel acknowledged his question with a nod and pulled in a ragged breath. "She and your grandfather were in an accident, Gabe, a really bad accident. And . . . and God took them to live with our father."

I heard gasps from Beth and Vera, but Gabe didn't say a word.

Gilly blinked hard, and her bottom lip quivered. She scooted off the love seat and ran to the window. "Is Mama in heaven with the angels now, too?" she asked, searching the sky.

Daniel nodded. "She is, Gilly."

She crawled back up beside him. "And Grandfather, too?"

He nodded again. "And Grandfather, too."

Gabe's eyes glistened with sudden understanding. He knew

what this news meant, but, like most kids, he had to make sure. "Then Mama won't be coming home tonight, will she?" he asked.

Daniel didn't answer. His face crumpled in pain, and his dreadful struggle twisted in my heart as well.

Gabe blinked, and tears rolled down his cheeks. "She won't be coming home *ever again*, will she?"

Daniel's eyes closed briefly, and he shook his head. "I'm sorry, Gabe," he whispered. "She'll be staying with Father now." He put his hands on their shoulders and leveled a fervent look at them. "But I don't want either of you to be afraid, do you hear me? Not ever, because I'll always be here. I'll never leave you."

"Mercy, neither?" Gilly asked.

Daniel glanced up at me and started to nod, but I stopped him with a tight shake of my head.

He frowned, clearly not understanding. "Well, I'm not sure," he said, stumbling over the words. "But . . . but I know she'll want to see you as much as she can."

"And don't forget me," Vera said. "I'll always be around when you need me."

"Me, too," Beth whispered.

The kids' faces puckered again, but they nodded and wiped at the new flood with the backs of their hands.

I sat back down beside them, aching to take their pain away. When they finally looked up again, they must've seen the same dark fear and worry in their big brother's face that I did.

Gilly climbed into his lap and laid her head against his

chest. Gabe scooted closer and twined his little arm around Daniel's.

After a moment, Daniel's head dropped and his shoulders shook. He grabbed up the kids in a fierce hug and buried his wet face in their hair.

"You'll *always* have me," he whispered to them. "Always."

"You don't have to be afraid of change.
You don't have to worry about what's been taken away.
Just look to see what's been added."

JACKIE GREER

chapter
32

I was thankful to see Christmas Day coming to a close. I'd moved through the evening like I was under a spell, doing what I could to ease the kids' loss, but Daniel had been what they needed most. He sat on the love seat with them, reading, till their eyelids drooped and closed, then carried them up, one at a time, and tucked them into bed.

The stories had helped, but tomorrow would likely be just as difficult for them. For Daniel, too.

I felt numb, strangely empty of tears and regrets. My mind jumped from guns to Mama's teacups, bloody clothing to Charity's Christmas garlands, then splintered into fragments so vague and elusive I'd forget what I was doing.

With great difficulty, I pushed myself into the kitchen to make mugs of warm cider. My hands moved almost on their own, going from one familiar motion to another, till I could finally bring my thoughts around to now, this minute, and what was coming.

When Daniel came back downstairs, we sat by the fire, watching flames dance. I didn't know how to tell him that I'd be leaving soon, but it was he who brought up the subject first.

"What happened earlier?" he asked. "You're not really thinking of quitting, are you?"

I knew this talk was inevitable, but now that we'd begun, all I wanted was for it to be over. "I have to," I said finally.

He gave me a dazed and puzzled look. "I can keep paying you, Mercy. I can even give you a raise."

"It's not the money, Daniel. I just can't live here alone with you now that Mrs. Wilder's gone. What would people say?"

He shook his head. "I don't care what they say. You love the kids—I know you do—and they love you."

It was true. From the first time I saw them, they felt like family, like maybe I still had a small piece of Justice and Honor with me. But surely Daniel understood what gossip could do. Girls who live with men they aren't married to are considered sullied, unclean. No one wants them after that, not for employment and certainly not for marriage. Regardless of how respectably I conducted myself, if I lived here with Daniel, I'd end up with a life far worse than Mama's ever was. I was trapped. I couldn't stay, but I didn't want to go, either.

I set my untouched mug on the side table. "You know I don't want to lose the kids, Daniel." I gave him a hopeful glance. "If it's okay with you, I could still help out for a while, so you could keep working. I could be here before breakfast and leave when you get home."

He tossed me a sour look. "It wouldn't be the same."

"I know."

"Then stay. The kids just lost their mother, Mercy. They'll

do better knowing you're here every night." He looked up at me, eyes pleading. "I will, too."

He was afraid. I could hear it in his voice, see it in his face. The thought of raising two kids alone worried him. I didn't blame him, but I was scared, too. Scared of what staying would do to my life, and even more frightened of leaving. What would I do when I couldn't come back here again?

It was an impossible situation. I closed my eyes in a futile attempt to settle my pitching stomach, then gathered what little courage I had to stand. "I'm sorry, Daniel," I whispered. "I really have no choice. I need to get my things."

"You're going now? Tonight?"

I nodded. "But I'll be back in the morning, if that's okay. I know you still have funeral arrangements to make."

He stared at me, stunned, and guilt prickled through me. "Yeah, sure," he said, throwing up his hands. "Thanks."

I headed to my room to pack up my rose-print flour sack, leaving Daniel muttering behind me. I was sick at the thought of leaving him, but glad I couldn't hear his mumbled comments. The angry words would surely tumble around in my head forever.

THE MOON HADN'T risen yet, but here I was again, alone on another road, this time with only stars to light the way to Emma's. Somehow leaving had become an inescapable part of my life, but what followed was always worse. Like never seeing Mama, Papa, and the kids again. Or the Bonners. It was an anguish that haunted everything I did, stalked me every step I took. I didn't see how I would ever make peace with it.

Now I was facing it again. Mrs. Wilder was gone, and I'd surely lose Daniel and the kids, too. No matter how much I wanted to continue working for them, I couldn't. I couldn't keep imposing on Emma, either, asking her to provide me with a place to sleep every night. I had only one alternative, and just thinking of it sent a wave of nervous dread through me. I'd have to find new employment—a live-in position—and, like before, I'd have to find it soon.

I saw a light through the front door of the Glory. Someone was still up. I walked around back to the kitchen and knocked.

Emma peered out the window, then swung the door wide. "Come in out of the cold," she said.

Her voice sounded strained and tired. No doubt Mrs. Wilder's death had been hard on her. I hated to burden her further, but I didn't have anyplace else to go. "I'm sorry it's so late," I said, pushing the door closed behind me.

She shrugged. "I couldn't sleep anyway. After the day we had, all kinds o' things been swarmin' in my head like bees."

"Would you mind if I stayed awhile?"

"Well, now, you already know I wouldn't."

"Thank you." I sank into a chair. "And please thank Beth and Vera for me, too. I know their Christmas dinners were ruined."

"No need a-worryin'. Here, let me take that coat for you." Emma pulled it off and hung it on a hook by the door. "You look tired, Mercy. Why don't I make you some of that spiced tea you like? I got leftover duck and stuffing, too. Did you ever get to eat?"

"No, but I'm not hungry, Emma. Some of your good tea sounds real nice, though. Thank you."

While she fussed over the stove, I thought about all that had happened today. My head had been buzzing, too. It was almost too much for one soul to sort out. Had Mr. Collier really killed his own wife and son? Beaten them to death, then claimed they were trampled by a horse and wagon? The ugly thought churned up all kinds of vile images, including that of Mr. Collier lying limp and broken on the ground. I knew what Mama would've said, of course.

"An eye for an eye," I whispered.

"What's that?" Emma asked.

I gave her a long look, wondering if I should tell her about Devon, though, thinking back on all she'd said to me, she'd most likely figured it out years ago.

"Did Daniel tell you how Mrs. Wilder and her father came to die today?" I asked.

She slid one of the steaming mugs in front of me and sat down. "It was an argument over the eighty acres Sam left her, wasn't it?"

I nodded, and my belly gave a sudden nervous twitch. "But that wasn't all of it, Emma."

Her eyes narrowed. "What else?"

I peered up at her. "Fifteen years ago, Mr. Collier killed his wife."

She didn't even blink.

"Seems he wanted her inheritance for himself, a farm her father left her. I guess they argued over it, like he did today with his daughter." I tossed Emma a fretful glance, but her face was blank. "Mrs. Wilder was just a girl back then, but she saw it all. And that black button? That button came off Mr. Collier's coat when he was beating his wife and—"

"And Cora found it in her dead mother's hand. I always suspected as much," Emma said.

I glanced at her again, uneasy at the rigid way she sat in her chair and the sharp steel in her eyes. "There's more," I said.

She gave me the barest of nods, as if she'd known all along there would be.

"He beat your Devon, too, Emma," I said as gently as I could.

Her hands trembled around her mug, and I braced to tell her the rest. "I'm so sorry, Emma, but it appears Mr. Collier killed Devon the same way he killed his wife."

Emma closed her eyes for a long moment, and tears trickled down her cheeks.

"You knew all along, didn't you?" I asked.

She nodded. "Couldn't prove it, though."

I put my hand over hers. "I'm really sorry."

"No need." She brushed away the tears. "Mr. Collier ended up in the dirt, the same way he left my Devon." She let loose a bitter laugh and looked heavenward.

"He was trampled by horses, Devon! Did you hear that?"

She sighed. "Devon used to say, 'What goes over the devil's back always comes round under his belly.' Oh, and it did do that, didn't it?" Her face twisted into a strange mixture of grief and victory. "That shameful old coot shoulda known he'd get his one day."

I rubbed at my fingers, still feeling the sticky red blood that had coated them earlier. "I just wish he hadn't taken Mrs. Wilder with him."

"Yeah, me, too, Mercy. Cora deserved better. All three of 'em did, but it's best put behind us now." She shrugged. "The only good part 'bout this whole thing is seein' that buzzard six feet under, where he can't feed on no one else. Maybe now we can finally forget he ever drew breath."

She stared into her tea for a long moment, then looked up at me as if she'd already let the past go. "How'd it go with Daniel and those poor babes?" she asked.

Daniel. I flashed back on this evening, remembering the tenderness he'd shown the kids, the way he'd protected them, the fierce way he'd loved them, and a dizzy longing rushed at me. I stared at Emma. What had she asked me? I sat up straight, while uncertainty tumbled in my head. "Daniel is really good with those kids," I mumbled. "It's easy to see why they love him so."

She gave me a penetrating look, as if she'd read something between my words I hadn't known was there. I sat, filled with a prickly confusion, waiting for her to speak. Fortunately, she didn't pursue the odd thoughts I'd seen mirrored in her face.

"I'm sure they'll be fine," she said. "We always worry, but kids handle life and death better'n grown-ups most times. They're like weeds. Nothin' holds 'em back for long." She took a sip of her tea, studying me over the rim of her cup. "I was a bit surprised to see you tonight," she said. "I reckon Daniel's feelin' a tad edgy 'long 'bout now, takin' care of those two little ones all by hisself. I bet he misses you."

I squirmed, feeling as if I was back in the parlor all over again, flinching from Daniel's betrayed looks, struggling to explain myself. "I guess he's not very happy with me right now," I told her. "He didn't want me to leave." I glanced up at her, pleading to be understood. "But I just couldn't stay, Emma. You know that, don't you?"

She grunted her disapproval and gave me a wistful look. "No matter how right we might be with the Lord, Mercy, we still gotta live our lives for all the gossipy old biddies in town. Sad state, ain't it?" she asked. "Especially when it's clear you and Daniel should be raisin' those kids together."

I stared at her, surprised. She didn't know. I guess I never told her how I felt, how I'd done everything I knew to guard myself against being trapped by marriage like my mama was. "Oh, Emma," I said, shaking my head, "that's not going to happen."

She tossed me a skeptical frown. "Well, I don't see why not. You're old enough, better'n seventeen, and I seen the way that boy looks at you." She pointed a finger at me. "And don't you try to tell me you ain't crazy about them three yourself, 'cause no one talks like you do 'less'n they are."

Exasperation twitched inside me. "I'm not love-struck, Emma. I just care about them, and caring doesn't mean I want to spend the rest of my life cleaning up after them. Besides, I have no desire to marry and end up like my mama did, birthing baby after baby and working hard every day of my life for nothing."

"We all work hard, Mercy. That's just the way it is."

"Not for everyone. Some women are lucky enough to find out what makes them happiest, and then the work *isn't* hard anymore." I aimed a defiant glare at her. "And that's just what I plan to do, Emma. Find out what makes me happiest. Why should I settle for marriage like my mama did and spend my whole life following a husband farm to farm, cooking and cleaning and praying for just one good crop? None of us kids even went to school, Emma. If it hadn't been for Mama's home schooling, I would've been as ignorant as dishwater."

"Well, now," she said slowly. "And just who said your mama never found what made her happiest?"

Confusion skipped through me. "What?"

Emma leaned back in her seat and gave me a squint-eyed look, reminding me of her talent for sizing up everything and everybody. I suddenly felt like a befuddled hen with its neck stretched over a chopping block.

"It's a wonder you can walk straight, with that big ol' chip on your shoulder," she said.

"It's not a chip," I said, frustration crawling all over me. "I just know what I don't want, that's all."

Emma gave me an unhurried nod. "Sure sounds like you do. So have you given any thought to what you *do* want?"

I tipped up my mug and went to the sink. "Some," I said over my shoulder, still annoyed with her.

"Well, Mercy, you might oughta try a bit harder. Last time I looked, Daniel ain't never had to move farm to farm to make a living."

I stared at her, still too mired in muddy uncertainty to speak.

"I think I'll just go fetch your quilts now," Emma said. With a sly grin, she carried her mug to the sink and headed upstairs.

chapter
33

I GUESS I'VE never known what made Mama happiest, but she surely couldn't have found it living the way she did all those years. Still, there was a ring of truth in Emma's words that scared me at first. She'd made it sound as if Mama's legacy was as inevitable as dying, like marriage was the only choice open to me and I'd never find out what would make me happiest.

Somehow I'd have to prove her wrong.

I spread my quilts on the floor of the storeroom and dressed for bed. It'd been a long, horrible day. All I wanted now was to lose myself in sleep, but I couldn't seem to stop thinking about what Emma said. She'd definitely been right about one thing. Daniel was different from Papa. He didn't have to worry about boll weevils or drought or whether he'd have enough food to last the winter. Whoever married Daniel would have an easier life than Mama had, but it would always be more of the same. A woman's life never changed. Every single day would bring the same chores, the same hunger for what might've been. Only the number of babies changed.

I curled up on my pallet, thinking again of Mama. Though she'd never asked, she must've always known I wanted more out of life. And now Emma, with her café and her hard-earned independence, would have to realize that, too.

I pulled my quilt up under my chin, grateful that at least some of what Emma had set spinning in my head appeared to be back in its place. I was tired, too tired to keep rehashing what I already knew, and drained from the endless death and grief and goodbyes.

I closed my eyes and felt myself drifting off, barely aware that my thoughts had slipped into something dark and menacing. But it was already too late. Dreams of hooves and guns and blood-soaked clothing chased me till my quilts lay twisted at the foot of my pallet. I woke, cold and shivering, and pulled the covers back up, only to find them tossed aside again later.

Long before morning, I finally gave up on sleep, refusing to dream again, and lay in the dark till a sliver of light from the kitchen lit the shelves of canned tomatoes, corn, and black-eyed peas.

Emma had begun her day, and still I lay quietly. I closed my eyes, taking comfort in the sounds of her lighting the stove and in the soft shuffling of her shoes across the cold floor. It reminded me of home, of Mama.

I'd grown up with those sounds, and even if it was just for a moment, I wanted to believe that when I opened my eyes again I'd see Mama making breakfast for Papa and all us kids. I'd stretch and look through the loft railing at her, and she'd smile up at me with a finger to her lips, warning me to not wake

Honor. Then she'd pull out her big bowl and start mixing up biscuits or pancakes. She never seemed to mind getting up before everyone else. In fact, I couldn't remember hearing a single complaint from her about having to do any of the chores I'd found so boring and tiresome.

My eyes popped open.

For the first time, I realized I'd never questioned why that was. Not even once.

I heard the kitchen door open and close. Emma had left to fetch bacon and ham from the smokehouse. I needed to leave, too. Daniel had funeral arrangements to make today for Cora and her father, and I wanted to be with Gabe and Gilly. No one could ease their loss, but I could at least dry the tears and make sure they knew how much their mother loved them. They needed to remember that.

I rolled up my pallet, dressed for the day, and found Emma back in the kitchen when I came out, packing up a basket of food.

"Heading out early?" she asked.

I nodded. "Daniel agreed that I could work days till I find another position. I hope to be out of your way before too very long."

"You're hardly in the way, Mercy." She spread a towel over the food and handed me the basket. "Take this with you. It's just a little somethin' to have on hand when people start droppin' in with condolences."

I stared at the bulging basket. "Thank you, Emma. I hadn't thought that far ahead."

"No trouble." She gave me a sideways glance. "I guess you ain't had a chance to mull over the talk we had last night?"

"Only a little, but I won't forget what you said."

"I'll settle for that." She looked satisfied, at least for the time being. "Now you get goin'. It'll be daylight soon, and heaven knows Daniel is gonna need you today."

I picked up the basket, thanked her again, and headed out the door. I felt a bit more confident than I had last night. I didn't have to be like Mama if I didn't want to, and Emma's nagging wasn't going to change my mind.

OVER THE NEXT few nights, Emma didn't bring up the subject of Daniel again, but I hardly slept anyway. I'd had no choice but to run the Wilder house as though it were my own, and when Daniel had to be away, I found myself in the odd position of greeting guests, serving them tea and cake, and accepting their condolences on his behalf. It was an uncomfortable role. Instead of watching from the corner of a room, I'd become a character in one of Charity's stories, someone I didn't really know, as if the real me had perished that day by the creek, too.

I attended the funeral, my attention solely on the children, wanting to give them all that Cora might have. When it was finally over, I came back to the house and served guests a midday meal, moving respectfully among them, smiling when acknowledged, inquiring after their needs when plates or glasses were empty.

At some point Emma pulled me aside and spoke to me, but I couldn't remember why. I realized later that it was she who stood beside me in the kitchen that evening, washing dishes, and it was she who drove me home in Cora's Ford and put me into her own bed. I glimpsed the setting sun from her window and marveled briefly that I'd never watched a sunset from bed before. And that was the last I remembered.

I woke the next day, startled at first to find myself in Emma's room, but even more so to find the sun straight over-head. I hurried to dress and ran downstairs.

"Well, look at you," Emma said, smiling. "All rested up?"

"Emma," I fussed, "you shouldn't have let me sleep so long. And in your own bed, too." Embarrassment at having forced her out of her bedroom made my cheeks flush hot.

"Oh, hush, now. It all worked out."

"What about Daniel and the kids?" I asked her. "Are they okay?" I felt lightheaded and confused. "I . . . I can't seem to remember."

"Of course you can't remember. You were half dead yourself when we brought you back here. We were gettin' scared we'd have to plan another funeral." She laughed and set a fat cinna-mon roll and a glass of milk in front of me. "Besides, it was Daniel who insisted I put you to bed. He said to tell you he'd take care of the kids."

"Oh." For a moment I was even more baffled. Daniel and I hadn't talked much for days, not since the evening I moved to Emma's. Had he decided to let me go?

Emma turned back to the stove, and I sat at the table, sipping my milk, thinking about that likelihood. The whole idea pushed me more off course than I thought possible, like I'd lost sight of shore and might never step foot on solid land again.

"'Twixt you and me," Emma said over her shoulder, "I think he could use some lookin' after. He had a pretty rough day yesterday."

I stared at her, taking note of the sudden glint in her eye.

"And," she continued, "since you appear all rested, seems you might wanna give him a bit of help 'fore the day is done."

She was matchmaking again. She reached for my coat and held it till I rose and slipped my arms into the sleeves.

"Here," she said, handing me my cinnamon roll. "You can eat this on the way."

I just stood there looking at her. Couldn't she see that I might not even be welcome at the Wilders'?

"Well, go on," she said, pushing me out the door. "Get on over there."

I watched the door close in my face, and though I tried, I couldn't seem to move. I felt as though I'd been plucked up by the scruff of my neck and left dangling above the earth with no clear place to put my feet. I turned to look about me. The steps, the burning barrel, Emma's kitchen—it was all so familiar, but it wasn't home. It would never be home.

Slowly I walked around the building and started on my way. The road crunched beneath my shoes, setting up a rhythm my heart wasn't in step with. Seems I'd walked a lot these past months, going wherever life pushed me as if I had no will of my own, and now I was headed blindly toward another familiar place, another place I couldn't call home.

Once more God had turned a page in my book, but for the life of me, I couldn't read a single word.

chapter 34

DANIEL WAS HALFWAY up the stairs, taking the kids to their room for an afternoon nap, when he hollered for me to come in. Apparently, he hadn't expected me. The house was already neat and orderly.

"I want Mercy," Gilly said when she saw me.

Gabe nodded. "Me, too."

I waited, uneasiness crawling all over me. Daniel nodded, but it was impossible to discern how he really felt about my being there. I took Gilly's hand, and, once upstairs, I pulled off shoes and tucked quilts under chins while Daniel plucked a small book off a shelf. He thumbed to a well-worn page and read a silly poem that made the kids laugh.

"Now you can sleep with a smile on your face," he said. "Remember, though, that I'll be right downstairs, okay?"

"Mercy, too?" Gilly asked.

"I'll be here," I assured them. I waved from the doorway and followed Daniel downstairs to the parlor.

"I'm sorry I wasn't here earlier," I said, rubbing my sweaty palms against my skirt.

He shook his head. "Emma was supposed to let you sleep. Why did you come?"

I cringed at the thorns in his question. He was still angry. Maybe he *did* want me gone. "I just wanted to help, if that's okay." I peered at him, tangled in a sudden breathless fear. "Do you still want me to take care of the kids during the day?"

"Yeah, sure," he said with a shrug, and turned to inspect the Christmas tree.

My pent-up breath escaped in a low *whoosh*. My feet were back on firm ground.

"I was thinking of getting rid of this thing," he said, pointing to the tree. "It's only a reminder, you know?"

I nodded, glad to have something to do. I began removing Mrs. Wilder's special ornaments and placing them in the tissue-lined box that Daniel had set on the parlor table. He gathered the snowflake garland and carefully folded it into a flat bundle. I watched with surprise as he wedged it beside the ornaments and closed the lid.

"We'll keep it for next year," he said.

I smiled, but his words had brought home what I hadn't fully accepted till now. I wouldn't be here next Christmas, and that inescapable fact hit me like a slap.

I watched him carry the bare tree through the kitchen doorway, feeling as if my heart had been uprooted as well. With things the way they were, there wasn't much I could do about it. I fetched the broom to sweep up stray pine needles, and without a word or a glance my way, Daniel gathered up the embroidered skirt that had covered the floor beneath the tree. The distance between us was still growing.

I emptied the dustpan, and when I came back, I found Daniel standing in the middle of the room, holding a white box tied with red ribbon.

He shrugged and held it out to me. "I guess it got pushed behind Cora's chair. It's for you."

I stood there looking at it, unable to move.

"Open it," Daniel said. "She obviously wanted you to have it."

I took the package from him and sat on the edge of the love seat. *For Mercy, from Cora,* the folded card said. I opened it up and stared at the flowing script for a long moment.

"What does it say?" Daniel asked.

I found my voice and read it to him.

> *Dear Mercy,*
> *I've seen the love you've given my children,*
> *and it is with great gratitude that I share*
> *one of my mother's angels with you.*
> > *God's blessings,*
> > *Cora Wilder*

The words blurred. I wiped away tears and opened the box. A painted angel looked back at me. Hands trembling, I reached inside and held up the winged carving by its ribbon.

"She hardly knew me," I said with wonder.

I glanced at Daniel, waiting for him to say what seemed obvious to me. Surely he knew that I couldn't accept such a personal and cherished gift, yet he didn't say a word. "It . . . it must be a mistake," I told him. "Why would she give away something so beautiful and precious?"

"I think Cora came to love you like family." Daniel shot me a pointed look. "We all have."

I didn't know what to say. I started to place the angel back in the box and noticed something else inside. I pulled out a small diary. Unlike Charity's worn notebook, this one was covered in black leather, and my name had been engraved in gold letters on the front. I opened it and found another message from Mrs. Wilder, an inscription that read simply: *Now you can write your own story.*

Her words, so much like Mama's, shot through me lightning-quick. The empty box crashed to the floor.

Daniel picked it up. "What's wrong?" he asked with a frown.

My heart pounded, and for a moment I couldn't breathe. I shook my head, avoiding his eyes, and gave him a nervous laugh. "Nothing, Daniel. Really. I . . . I should put all this away."

I hurried to my room, pushed open the door, and just stood there.

What was I *doing*?

This wasn't my room anymore.

The never-ending loss bubbled up again and flooded down my cheeks. I slumped to the bed and buried my face in the pillow.

I SLEPT AGAIN and woke to find a blanket pulled up around my shoulders. The diary and angel lay on the bedside table. I rolled over and stared at the ceiling, not wanting to get up. I didn't want to face Daniel and the kids. I didn't want to see the disappointment in their eyes when I left after supper, but mostly I didn't want to go someplace new and start all over again.

Emma's words sounded in my head. "Have you given any thought to what you *do* want?" she'd asked.

I hadn't. All I knew was that I didn't want to end up like Mama. Did I?

How could it be that she'd never minded doing all the things I complained about? Her life had been full of dirty, boring work—work that never got finished. No one, not even Mama, could've been happy about that. Yet she never fussed.

I asked her once why she married so young, and she told me she'd loved Papa since she was a girl.

"He only got to go to school twice a week," she'd said. "He had to work hard to help out his family, but he studied nights and kept up with every student in that schoolhouse, including me. Now, tell me, Mercy," she'd said with a big smile, "how could I *not* love someone like that?"

By the time Mama was seventeen, she and Papa were married, and just before a year was up, I was born. I guess it never occurred to me to wonder why she took pleasure in cooking his favorite meals, or watched out the window every evening for him to come in from the fields, or made sure he got enough sleep at night.

I was wondering now, though. I suppose I took Papa's music for granted, too, but, oh, I did remember how Mama loved to hear him play his harmonica.

"I swear he can make it talk," she'd say. "If you listen close, Mercy, he'll play you a story from beginning to end."

Maybe I should've listened harder. Charity always sat at the table writing when he played. Maybe that's where she got her stories, straight from Papa's harmonica.

But why didn't Mama ever complain?

Even when diapers piled up and it was so cold the laundry wouldn't dry on the line, she still didn't grumble. She'd bring them in, half frozen, and hang them over chairs and from the loft railing, telling us kids, "We're setting sail, you landlubbers. Better find your sea legs!"

I smiled, thinking of how we'd all swayed to her imaginary waves till we were sure we'd see nothing but ocean if we looked out the window. And no one laughed harder than Mama.

I'd forgotten that.

I guess I'd forgotten a lot of things. Pondering it all now, I had to wonder if Mama might've gotten exactly what she wanted out of life. It didn't sound like much to me. A husband and kids, a little music and laughter. Could that've been all she really wanted?

So what about me? What did *I* want?

I closed my eyes, trying once more to figure that out, and heard Gabe and Gilly talking in the kitchen. I needed to get up.

"Nothing in life is to be feared.
It is only to be understood."

MARIE CURIE

chapter 35

THE MYSTERY OF MAMA flitted like blue jays in my head, calling me first to one memory, then another, but I didn't have time to think about all that now. It was late, and there was still supper to cook. I straightened the bed and found Daniel and the kids at the kitchen table, quietly practicing their numbers.

"Mercy, guess what," Gilly said. "I can count to ten!"

I listened while she recited her numbers and clapped when she was through, but Gabe wasn't about to be outdone.

"Yeah, but I can count to twenty—wanna hear?" he asked, not waiting for a reply.

I clapped again. The kids grinned with pride, but I couldn't bring myself to look at Daniel. I turned to the pantry instead. "Are you hungry?" I asked over my shoulder.

"No need to cook," Daniel said. "There's still so much in the icebox from yesterday."

"Then I'll get it all out, and we can have a picnic."

"Here?" Gilly asked.

"We *can't* have a picnic in the house, Mercy," Gabe said.

"Of course we can. We'll have our picnic in front of the fireplace. You two go upstairs and get a quilt, okay?"

Their eyes widened with new possibilities, and they scrambled up the back stairs to get the quilt. I put bowls of leftover roast pork and potatoes on the worktable and peered at Daniel from the corner of my eye. I'd been missing his easy smiles.

He looked up in time to see me studying him and turned abruptly toward the parlor. "I'll put another log on the fire," he said over his shoulder.

Chilled by his tone, I watched him go, all too aware of the growing bitterness inside him. He couldn't accept that I had to leave, and it had pushed a dark wall between us, thinned his smiles, and clouded his eyes. It had also left me with yet another wound, different from my recent sharp losses, but not any more likely to heal.

The kids came back down, dragging a quilt behind them. They spread it on the floor in front of the fire, then ran back to the kitchen to help.

"So what shall we see on our picnic?" I asked, filling their arms with plates and napkins.

They looked up at me, their eyes full of questions.

"Shall we go back to the woods where we cut down the tree, or would you like to go someplace new?"

"Ohhh," Gabe said. He leaned toward Gilly and whispered, "It's pretend."

"I know, I know!" she said, jumping up and down. "I wanna see the deers!"

"Yeah," Gabe said. "The meadow where we saw all the deer. That's a good place."

"Then that's where we'll go."

I watched them carry their plates into the parlor, and listened while they told Daniel where we were going for our picnic. He laughed, a sound I hadn't heard in a long while. I drank it in and framed the moment in my mind. I didn't want to forget.

THROUGH THE NEXT few months, I looked for work every Wednesday I was off, but Canton still hadn't shaken free of the losses that'd swept through its homes. I wondered if the rest of the world struggled with the same dark aftermath. Or, worse yet, perhaps the sickness was still out there, creeping into other towns, stealing into homes, robbing them of mamas and daddies and babies.

Clearly there was no work to be had here. Emma said it was a sign. She said that the good Lord was trying to tell me something and that I was just too stubborn to listen. There were times she got downright surly about it.

Of course, I knew what she wanted, and even though the talk we'd had about Daniel still haunted me now and then, I also knew I couldn't give Emma her wish.

I did continue working for Daniel, however, and his bitterness toward me slowly changed. I was grateful, but every day that passed brought me closer to them all, making it difficult to accept my pay without guilt and harder than ever to think of leaving them. I insisted that Emma take part of my wages for lodging, but she refused, saying, "Mercy, you can't hardly call sleeping on a pallet in the storeroom lodging."

Each day, I looked forward to seeing Gabe and Gilly, teaching their lessons, and dancing with them to the Victrola. We'd snuggle on the love seat where I'd read stories to them before supper, but what I loved most were the hugs, the way their little arms wrapped so tightly around my neck. They brought a sense of family back to me, and before I knew it, they'd even helped me attain a workable peace with God. It seemed impossible to hold on to old grudges when I was blessed with such sweet hugs every day.

Their favorite game was pretend. We'd roar like lions, swim with the whales, or scamper up trees like squirrels, and each evening as I left, I'd hear them telling Daniel about their newest adventure. It felt right, like I was meant to be part of their lives, and yet I knew someday I'd have to leave.

Sometimes when the kids napped, I'd open up my new diary and stare at the pages, waiting for inspiration. But no matter how hard I tried, I couldn't bring myself to write in it. My life was as blank as the pages in that book. I had no clear path ahead of me, and it seemed that, till there was one, I wouldn't be able to write a single word.

During those brief alone times, I'd read Charity's diary instead, only a line or two at first, and then in great gulps, laughing when she captured Justice's shines, and crying when she brought Honor so close I could almost breathe in the sweetness of her. It was a gift, difficult and sometimes painful to read, but one I would cherish always. Charity had given me a way to go home again.

THE WORST OF WINTER passed without snow, and by March, trees budded and grass greened. The city of Canton seemed to be blooming at last, too. Men had plowed and planted, children played ball on street corners, and on Friday, April 4, I finally found a position in a boardinghouse. I was expected to start work on Sunday morning.

The Carrington House wasn't as nice as the Wilders', but it was very large. Eight bedrooms, with as many boarders. Miss Carrington had taken the roomy attic for her quarters, and mine would be the small nook off the kitchen. It was bare except for a cot and chest—no pictures, no windows—and not much larger than a storeroom. In fact, I suspected that it had once *been* a storeroom and figured Emma would get a big laugh out of that. Yet it wasn't too bad. Most of my time would be spent in the large kitchen, anyway, cooking for boarders.

Miss Carrington was a tall, angular woman with a steely gaze that could cut right through a body if she was displeased. I noted, too, during our brief meeting, that she appeared to be the type who wasn't pleased often. I wondered if she'd given up on finding a husband and having a family of her own, or if she'd decided long ago to choose a different path, like me.

Whatever Miss Carrington's reason for not marrying, she didn't seem too happy with the outcome. She owned a large, comfortable house, bigger than anything Mama or I had ever dreamed of having, but I'd sensed a despair around her the instant I stepped through the door. I had to wonder how she'd arrived at such a bleak place in her life. It was almost as if the woman had chosen to be unhappy.

I hadn't thought much about Mama's heart signs for months, not since before Christmas, but something about my new employer reminded me that, like Mr. Bonner, she had to have a reason for the cold, stiff way she lived her life. I'd have to watch closely for signs in this woman if I was going to find a way to win her over. But first I'd have to tell Emma I'd be leaving. Then I'd have to face Daniel and the kids.

I decided to tell Emma my news just before she went to bed that night, thinking I could avoid her growls and scoldings. She went upstairs without a word, all right, but was back down again long before she usually started her day. I heard her banging around in the kitchen like she was after the devil himself. I cringed. No doubt she'd have plenty to say before I left this morning.

I dressed and eased into the kitchen, ignoring the surly look she flung my way. She grabbed two mugs of tea, shoved one into my hands, and said, "Sit. We need to talk 'fore you end up doin' somethin' daft today."

I opened my mouth to object, but one look at Emma's face was enough to back me up and sit me down.

"It's time you stopped bein' so scared," she said, dropping into the chair across from me.

I frowned at her, prickling with impatience. "I'm not scared of anything except being trapped like my mama. You know that."

"Ha," she said with barefaced irritation. "You ain't seen

trapped, girl. Just wait till you go to work for that Carrington woman."

"It's just a job, Emma. It's not marriage. As long as I keep *that* from happening, I'll be free to do anything I want." Why couldn't she see that?

"And just what would that be, missy?" She shot me a fierce look. "Leavin' those kids? Watchin' Daniel hire some ninny of a girl who won't give a fig for 'em? Is that what you want?"

I felt a pang of guilt, then utter frustration. "You know Daniel wouldn't let that happen. Besides, Gabe and Gilly are different. There's not a soul in this town who could keep from loving those kids. I certainly couldn't."

"Not everybody's like you, Mercy. Too bad you can't see that." She tipped up her mug and took a big gulp.

Well, there was one thing I *could* see. She hadn't been able to talk me into doing what she wanted, so now she was going to try bullying me into it. I gave her a hostile squint-eyed look. "Just tell me why you think I should spend my life raising someone else's kids when the very thing I don't want is marriage and family? For heaven's sake, Emma, I can barely take care of myself. What do you expect from me?"

"To go after what you *really* want, of course!"

A wrathy heat hit my cheeks. I flung up my hands. "And *you* know what that is better than I do?"

She slammed her mug on the table. "I surely do, Mercy Kaplan, and it ain't waitin' for you like buried treasure in no boardin' house!"

I stared at her, at the angry set of her jaw and the fire in her eyes. I'd had enough. I stood, too afraid to stay longer, too afraid that things might change between us forever if I did. Hands trembling, I took my mug to the sink. "I have to go, Emma," I said.

She didn't try to stop me, but as I stepped outside, I heard her whisper, "Oh, Mercy. Just *what* are you so scared of?"

chapter 36

EMMA THOUGHT I WAS SCARED? I pulled the door shut behind me, bristling at her words, and headed out to the road. Something about that last rebuke had reminded me of Mama. Emma had said it with a tired despair, the way I remembered Mama speaking when she thought that, no matter how many times she repeated something, I would never understand. Yet most times I did, though insight came slowly and usually left a sour taste in my mouth. Seems Mama had been right about a lot of things. A fact that made me wonder if Emma might be, too.

I grudgingly allowed myself to think about what she'd been trying to tell me, and finally I had to admit that maybe I *was* afraid. I was definitely afraid of boll weevils and raging epidemics that take food from children and rip loved ones from your arms and put them in the ground. Nothing in the world was safe from that kind of misery. Nothing. Yet I knew this wasn't all that Emma had been talking about. She thought I was scared of Daniel, of marriage, but she was wrong. Fear had nothing to do with my decision. Someday I might end up wanting marriage and all that comes with it, but not yet. Not before I was sure. And no one, not even Emma, was going to bully me into doing something I wasn't ready to do.

Still, I felt bad about walking out on her the way I had, especially after all she'd done for me. I didn't want to lose her friendship. Maybe it was a good thing this would be my last night at the Glory. Tomorrow I'd be sleeping at the Carrington House.

Locusts sang, birds twittered high in the trees, and cotton clouds lazed in a warm spring sky, but it did little to lighten my mood. I tried to let the bad feelings go and turn my thoughts to the future. Trouble was, I couldn't see much beyond today. I knew the Carrington House would be only a stepping-stone, which was fine with me. It would be a means to get me . . . get me . . . where? I blinked in the bright sunlight. I really didn't know yet, but surely that would come to me soon. I was looking for the good and trusting, like Mama told me to do, right?

Farther down the road, I saw an increasing number of wild-flowers—pink buttercups, Indian paintbrushes, bluebonnets—and I thought of Gabe and Gilly. They'd probably already seen them. I smiled, picturing the kids running from flower to flower, excited about taking home a big bouquet. I'd take them out soon, let them gather enough to fill vases for every room in the—

I stopped at the side of the road, too sick to take another step. This day would be my last with them, and I might not have even that, once Daniel knew about my new position.

It would be difficult to tell him. He'd never really understood that I couldn't stay nights at the house with them. And because I couldn't, I'd had to impose on Emma for months now. My only choice was employment that would provide me a place to sleep, and I'd been very lucky, finally, to find one.

I shuffled down the road, worried that maybe Daniel would be too angry to let me finish out the day. If so, I'd have to leave without sharing even one more meal with them. There'd be no games, no stories, no pretending.

A new realization stopped me again, and my heart thumped hard and heavy with the truth of it. There'd be no more long visits. Miss Carrington hadn't been as generous with time off as Mrs. Wilder had been. Cooking three meals every day for a houseful of people didn't leave much free time for anything else. The Glory had taught me that.

I groaned. What I'd dreaded all along was happening. It was real. Today was my last chance to be with them, and soon I'd be alone in that Carrington House, cooking for strangers that came and went. There'd be no Daniel, no laughter, no more little arms around my neck.

How had it come to this?

I headed down the road once more, regret squirming inside me.

Daniel was already frying bacon when I arrived. He looked up at me with his customary hello nod, and for a moment, something shifted in his expression, making me feel as if my news must show all over me. I guess he had something else on his mind, though. When Gabe and Gilly ran to meet me with their usual hugs, they couldn't stop chattering about how Daniel had promised to take them to gather wildflowers.

"We're gonna pick lots and lots of flowers," Gilly said.

Gabe nodded. "And we're gonna have a picnic, too, a real one this time," he said, laughing.

I tossed Daniel a questioning look, and a pink flush crept into his cheeks. "I don't have any work right now, and thought I might stay home with the kids. If you don't mind, that is."

My stomach knotted. "Of course I don't mind." I looked away, trying to hide my disappointment. "Then I guess you won't need me today."

"Yes, we will!" Gilly shouted.

"She *has* to go with us, right, Daniel?" Gabe asked.

I peered at Daniel, waiting, trying to remember to breathe.

He shrugged. "Looks like they want you to stay. Is that okay?"

The knots in my stomach turned to lively flutters. With a nod, I tied on my apron and pulled the fork from his hand. "Here," I managed to say. "I'll do that for you." My news would just have to wait awhile longer.

After breakfast, I mixed up a pound cake for the picnic, put it in the oven, and started my morning chores. While the house filled with the warm aroma of sweet butter and vanilla, I picked up toys, dusted, and made beds, making sure to smooth away the last of the wrinkles. I lingered in each room before moving on, uncomfortably aware that my melancholy was beyond foolish.

This was just a house. No doubt I'd care for many more in my lifetime.

It wasn't long before the kids caught up with me and followed me room to room, calling out questions like "Where does dust come from, Mercy?" and "Why does it turn into fuzz balls and end up under the bed?"

"It's hiding," I told them, "hoping to play with your toys while you're sleeping."

I listened to their laughter, but the sound only served as a dismal reminder. *Last time*, it whispered, and faded away.

I finished the chores and went back to the kitchen with the kids to make sandwiches. Daniel pulled the Ford around to the porch, which surprised me. "I thought we'd be walking only a short distance up the road," I told him.

He laughed. "They want 'lots and lots' of flowers. We'll probably have to cover the whole countryside. Besides, look at the size of that picnic basket."

He was right. I'd chipped ice from the icebox into a large jar of sweetened tea and wrapped it with towels to keep it chilled. It *was* big. And heavy. We also had the blanket and shallow buckets of cool water to keep the flowers from wilting. It was a lot to carry. With new appreciation for Mrs. Wilder's Ford, I helped Daniel load everything into the back, and we headed off to find flowers.

We stopped often, and at each new place I felt the minutes ticking away. While Gabe and Gilly scampered from one blossom to another, I sat on the bumper beside Daniel, but I couldn't bring myself to tell him about my new position. Not yet. It'd been such a long time since I'd seen him so happy, and I didn't want anything to spoil this last, perfect day.

Instead, Daniel told me how his father used to make fishing lures of cedar and feathers, and I told him about Charity's stories and how I hoped to have a place for Mama's china cups someday. He painted pictures of working side by side with his father on automobiles and wagons, and I helped him hear the sweet sounds that used to come from Papa's harmonica.

For a while I pushed my weighty chore aside, enjoying Daniel and the kids, assuring myself that there would be ample opportunity later for sharing my cheerless news.

Daniel drove for miles while the kids sang every song and nursery rhyme they could remember. Their little voices mangled some of the verses so crazily, Daniel had a hard time stifling his laughter. I listened and watched, wanting to remember.

Finally, he pulled off the road near an open meadow awash with black-eyed Susans. In the distance, I saw deer nibbling tender grasses along the tree line and wondered if this was the place Mrs. Wilder had loved.

"Gabe, you carry the blanket," Daniel said, "and I'll get the basket."

"Can we pick more flowers?" Gilly asked.

"I don't know where you'll put them," Daniel said, "but maybe, after we eat."

I smiled, watching him puzzle over the best way to get the

picnic basket out, approaching the problem with the same attention he seemed to give everything. He eased the buckets of flowers aside, taking care not to crush them, and pulled the heavy basket over their delicate blooms. I guess I'd never given this tenderness in Daniel much thought before now, but because I knew I'd probably never see him again like this, it had become important, one more thing I wanted to carry away with me when I left.

We spread our blanket under a grove of trees just to one side of the meadow and attacked the basket of food. When every crumb was gone, Daniel and I lay down to rest our full bellies, with Gabe and Gilly between us. We stared through leaves to the blue sky above, listening to breezes whisper through branches, and soon Gilly's eyes closed. I closed my eyes, too, drinking in the sweetness of the moment, trying to assure myself that today's long goodbye would be enough.

I needed to remember that when I left them this evening I'd be taking the first step toward my future, my very own dreams, whatever they might be. I didn't know one other girl my age who could say that.

Gilly squirmed next to me in her sleep. She felt so small and vulnerable. I cuddled her baby softness closer to me, hoping that she and Gabe would continue to feel safe and loved when I was gone.

Branches tossed high in the trees, and leaves rustled. After a while I heard Gabe say, "The wind sounds like music," and that was the last I remembered.

I WOKE WITH A START to find Daniel's arm stretched behind the kids' heads and his hand tangled in my hair. For a moment I lost myself in the feel of his fingers against my cheek, though I knew it was foolish of me. I finally eased his hand away and sat up. The sun had almost disappeared behind the trees. We'd been asleep for hours.

I shook Daniel, then turned to the kids. "Wake up! We've slept the day away. We need to pack and get home."

The kids sat up and rubbed their eyes.

Daniel roused with a groan, but I caught his crooked grin. He hadn't minded this at all.

Gilly pointed at my tangled hair and giggled. "Look, Gabe. Daniel and Mercy falled asleep just like us."

My face flushed hot, but I ignored the embarrassment and packed up the basket. My thoughts had already turned to the unpleasantness that lay ahead. The knots of worry had begun to tighten.

When we got home, I helped the kids arrange vases of flowers all over the house. I especially loved the black-eyed Susans, which Mama had gathered only last spring to brighten our small cabin. I placed large bowls of them in the parlor and dining room, knowing they'd easily survive into next week, but knowing, too, that none of this was more important than telling Daniel and the kids about my leaving.

The weight of my mission continued to grow, harder to carry and impossible to put down. I felt it slowing my steps, tangling my thoughts, and still I dallied, putting off what I most needed to do.

Daniel went to the barn to take care of Mr. Collier's horses, and Gabe and Gilly ran upstairs to paint pictures of our picnic. I stood in the kitchen, watching them all go, and after a moment, the house grew still. I looked around me, full of dread, wishing the kids would thunder down again, bursting with laughter and questions, hands messy with paint. But the stairs were empty and quiet.

I finally had to turn away and start supper. Yet, even as I moved around the kitchen I'd come to know so well, my dark task followed me like a ghost.

I set the table and took my place with Daniel and the kids to eat, peering up at them often, trying to figure out the best way to tell them of my new position, but I just couldn't get past the whirlwind in my head. It scattered my thoughts so fast I couldn't hang on to a single word long enough to get anywhere. By the time Daniel was ready to read their Bible story, I was frantic with worry, and yet there I was in the kitchen, washing dishes. *Why?*

Guilt lurched inside me. There was no way around it. Come tomorrow, Daniel would pay for my cowardice. He'd have to tell Gabe and Gilly himself.

Without warning, a sudden tightness in my chest sucked my breath away, then swelled into wrenching sobs. I leaned hard against the sink. These children had already lost so much. How could I have done this to them? I imagined the hurt in

259

their faces when they woke to find me yanked from their lives, just like their mama and daddy had been, and then I glimpsed my life without their laughter, their hugs. More tears rained into the sudsy water.

After a long moment, I gulped air and wiped my eyes. I had to stop. Daniel would be down soon, and even though I'd failed at telling the kids, I *had* to tell him.

I pulled myself up and washed my face, and when I'd finished cleaning the kitchen, I looked around the room for the last time. Everything was back in its place.

Still shaky, I plucked up what was left of my courage and sat in the parlor to wait for Daniel. Moments later, he came downstairs, smiling, carrying something small in his hand. I gave him a quizzical look, and he held up a wrapped box.

"It's something I've wanted to give you for some time now, but until today, I had no hope you'd accept."

I stared at him, blinking, and for a moment I slipped into that dark place inside me, the place Mama's words never reached. I felt it push me toward the door, but when I looked into Daniel's eyes, I knew I couldn't run away. I had to stay. I had to tell him about tomorrow.

"Please," he whispered, folding my fingers around the tiny box. "Open it."

I didn't know what to do, other than fumble my way through the shiny paper and open the lid.

I gave Daniel a startled glance. On a bed of black velvet lay a ruby ring.

"My mother's wedding ring," he said.

I thought my heart would stop.

He sat on the love seat beside me, his green eyes soft in the firelight. "I knew almost from the first time I met you that I'd give you this ring," he said. "I saw who you were that night Gabe was lost, the way you carried him, the way you came back to help me. I saw how you never complained about being alone, even though you'd lost your whole family. I watched you help Cora, despite what you feared she'd done, and, oh, Mercy, just look at how Gabe and Gilly love you. You made stars and snowflake garlands, and you turned the kids into airplanes and birds!" He laughed and looked at me with amazement. "How do you do that?" He reached for my hand and cradled it in his. "And how could I *not* love someone like that?"

I stared at him while Mama's old words about Papa echoed in my head. I felt the horrible irony of it tremble through me and land with a thud at the bottom of my stomach.

I pushed the ring back at him. "Daniel, I can't." My news escaped in a breathy whoosh. "I've accepted another position. I start tomorrow."

He stared at me for longer than I thought I could bear, then slowly pulled away. "And this is what you really want?"

My answer tangled in my throat. I nodded, too sick to speak, too sick even to breathe.

I just couldn't be like Mama.

"The world is round and the place which may seem like the end may also be the beginning."

IVY BAKER PRIEST

chapter

37

SHADOWS HAD DEEPENED long before I left Daniel, and on my way back to town, I welcomed the peace and solitude that darkness brought. I sat on a bench near the courthouse, unwilling to face Emma. When I was sure she'd gone to her room, I slipped through the kitchen door and went to bed. I planned to leave again before she came down in the morning, hoping that, one day soon, she'd accept that I had to live my life the way I saw fit.

I tried hard to sleep, knowing my first day at work tomorrow would be difficult, but nothing seemed to quiet the ruckus in my head long enough to let that happen. Thoughts flitted from Mama to Emma to Miss Carrington and back again, but they always ended up with Daniel and the kids. I didn't know how to close my heart to them, and it was becoming painfully clear that I might never be able to do so.

Before daylight, I sat on the Carrington porch with my rose-print flour sack, waiting for six o'clock. This was the hour when Miss Carrington had wanted me to begin breakfast. She expected me to serve the meal at seven sharp, which worried me a bit. After all, I'd be working in a strange kitchen, and I didn't even know what she wanted to serve. I went over the possible menus, planning ahead for the best way to get it all done on time, and heard the town clock strike six.

I found Miss Carrington exactly as she'd been when I met her on Friday—prim and cold—with today's menu clutched in her hand. She handed it to me, checked her watch, and told me I'd find everything I needed in the kitchen. Then she turned and left.

Once in the kitchen, I took a quick look at the menu. Grits, toast, a slice of ham, and a soft-boiled egg for each boarder. That would be easy enough. I looked around, opening cupboards, checking the icebox, acquainting myself with the whereabouts of everything, and then got started.

Miss Carrington didn't bother with introductions that morning, but several of the boarders took time to state their names politely and inquire of mine. By the time I'd gotten through three full meals, I'd heard no complaints, but Miss Carrington had no praise, either. She simply handed me the next day's menu and said good night.

I hurried to finish up supper dishes and mop the floor, anxious to put my first day behind me. It had been long and tiring, but mostly it had been bare of the small pleasures I'd always found with Miz Beulah, Emma, and the Wilders. What worried me most was that I saw no promise for better days to come.

I hung up my wet cup towel and turned out the light, but I couldn't seem to move. I just stood there in the dark while all the old doubts I'd tried so hard to drown floated to the surface again. I thought I'd gotten past all that. After all, this was freedom, right? The very thing I'd fought so hard to keep.

I closed my eyes a moment, trying to overcome the roiling uncertainties, but instead of assurances, I saw only Gabe and Gilly. I flinched, remembering my cowardice, hating that they'd awakened this morning to find I wouldn't be back. And now I was scared for them, just like Emma knew I'd be, worried that whoever cared for them next might not read to them, or fly with them, or just plain hug them enough so they'd never be afraid. Emma was smart that way. She'd probably always listened to her heart.

So why couldn't I hear mine? Mama had said to watch for signs, not just in others, but in myself, too, and they'd show me the way. I tried to see what my heart was showing me, but all I saw was the pain I'd brought to Daniel's face when I'd refused his ring. The strange thing was, I'd felt that same pain. The very same. Thinking about it now, though, I didn't see how that could be. Unless . . .

Truth slid through the confusion inside me and anchored itself, like it had no intention of being pushed aside again. I stared at it with surprise. I'd actually wanted to say *yes* to Daniel. I'd wanted to make Gabe and Gilly my own and never leave Daniel's side.

I leaned hard against the worktable, trembling under the weight of this new certainty. Even now, just thinking of him set up a longing in me I'd never expected to feel, a longing so beautiful, yet so agonizing, it made me wonder. Was *this* what Mama felt for Papa? She could've had an easier life, a more exciting life, and yet she chose exactly what I'd walked away from. *Why?*

It seemed that if I was ever to know my own heart, know what was right for me, I'd have to understand hers first. Or at least try.

I closed my eyes again, thinking of Mama, sensing a surprising kinship with her. Perhaps it was because of my feelings for Daniel. Or maybe she and I were just more alike than I ever thought possible. I could almost see myself in her shoes, almost feel what she must've felt all those years.

After only a few moments, one thing became clear. Whether her hands were red and sore from doing laundry, or kneading bread dough, or helping Papa in the fields, I'd never seen a longing in her to be anyplace else. Her smile had held every monster at bay, her arms had stretched wide enough to encircle us all, and even when she hummed softly to only herself, her sweet contentment had found us, soothing away each fear, each worry.

Mama had been happy.

Despite what I might've thought, she'd found her happiness in Papa and us kids, and no amount of hard work had changed that. I opened my eyes and looked around the gloomy kitchen. Had I found mine?

That black question followed me through the dark and into my room. I tried to put it out of my mind, but as I pulled on my gown and crawled under the covers, another joined it. *Just what are you so scared of?* I heard Emma ask again.

I felt brief moment of irritation, but that old question just wouldn't go away. It shifted inside me, searching, turning locks, opening unfamiliar doors. I stared at my tiny room, felt its breathless walls closing in, felt the pressing weight of strangers sleeping on the floors above me.

"It's this," I whispered to Emma, finally understanding. "This is what I'm afraid of."

I guess she'd known all along that I'd accepted a bleak, loveless life for myself and that I'd allowed fear and circumstance to make that choice for me. And now *I* knew. This kind of freedom wasn't what I wanted at all. I wanted Daniel.

What had I done? Regret twined so tight around my heart I was sure I'd never get rid of it this time. I squeezed my eyes shut, more afraid than ever.

Like Emma, I guess Mama had seen fear in me, too. She knew I'd try to live my life by it, knew I'd make irrevocable mistakes. *It's up to each of us to get shed of old regrets and watch for the good coming*, she'd tried to tell me that long-ago day. I didn't understand it then. And even now doubt rose inside me, high as a mountain.

"But, Mama," I whispered into the dark, "what if I'm not like you? You found good in everything, even frozen diapers."

I flung back my covers. How did she *do* that? How did she make something out of nothing, turn music into stories and diapers into sails? It was like all the bad that happened to her disappeared with each sunrise, like she made up her whole life one day at a time, exactly the way she wanted it to be. Just dreamed it up and wrote it down, the way Charity wrote her stories.

The way Charity wrote.

I sat up, breathless with discovery.

Write it yourself, Mama had said.

Why hadn't I seen it before?

Mama had always known her own heart. And when God turned another page in her book, she didn't stare at the big empty expanse, waiting for words to appear.

She wrote on it.

I SLEPT. Without dreams and without even knowing when I had drifted off. I woke to a sensation of breathless flight, as though I'd been soaring, high and unfettered in a wide blue sky. I lay very still, trying to hold on to the feeling. Little by little, it slipped away, but not before leading me to a new and irrefutable conclusion.

I stuffed my belongings back into the rose-print flour sack, everything except Mrs. Wilder's gift. I found my pen and turned to the first page of the leather-bound diary.

Monday, April 7, 1919
Last night I remembered Mama, and I finally
understood what she'd known all along. We'd always
been alike, she and I.
    I can't hold back plagues of influenza any more
than she could hold back boll weevils, but, like Mama,
I can make sails out of diapers if I want.
    I can make sails.

ACKNOWLEDGMENTS

My deepest gratitude to the friendly people of Canton, Texas: the Canton Chamber of Commerce and Public Library, the Van Zandt County Courthouse and Van Zandt County Genealogical Society, the *Canton Herald* and the Van Zandt *County Line*. Special thanks to the gracious Mr. Starr, Postmaster Carol Franks, and especially to Mary Lynn Baugh of Hilliard's Furniture and Appliance for generously sharing her family history. Also, for exceptional insight, my thanks to my daughter, Aliisa, and husband, Wendel, and my writer friends Julie Hannah, Heather Miller, Kay Butzin, Woody Davis, and Barton Hill. And as always, heartfelt appreciation to my incomparable editor, Reka Simonsen.

By Marian Hale

The Truth About Sparrows

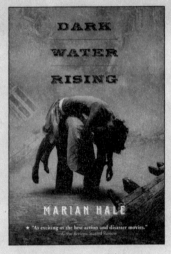

Dark Water Rising

The Goodbye Season